Fables, Fairies & Folklore

OF NEWFOUNDLAND

D1617446

Fables, Fairies & Folklore

OF NEWFOUNDLAND

by
Alice Lannon
and
Michael McCarthy

Jesperson Press Ltd.
1991

Jesperson Press Ltd.
39 James Lane
St. John's, Newfoundland
A1E 3H3

Text Design: Shellie Dawe
Cover and Layout Design: Pennylee Dawe
Typesetting & Printing: Jesperson Press Ltd.

The publisher acknowledges a financial contribution of the *Cultural Affairs Division* of the *Department of Culture, Recreation and Youth* of the Government of Newfoundland and Labrador which has helped make this publication possible.

Appreciation is also expressed to the *Canada Council* for its assistance in publishing this work.

Canadian Cataloguing in Publication Data

Lannon, Alice, 1927-

    Fables, Fairies and Folklore

    ISBN 0-921692-01-3

1. Legends — Newfoundland.   I. McCarthy, Michael J., 1932-   II. Title.

GR113.5.N5L36 1991   398.23'2718   C91-097542-6

Contents

Dedicated to our grandmother

Mary (Strang) McCarthy

SECTION ONE

Folktales

The following three folktales, "Open, Open Greenhouse", "Big Black Bull of Hollow Tree", and "Jack, Bill and Tom, and The Ship that Could Sail Over Land and Water", were told to us as children by our grandmother, Mary (Strang) McCarthy. As a little girl in Lawn, Placentia Bay she had been told these stories by an elderly aunt who was born in Lawn around 1820. This means that these stories have been passed on orally in our family for more than one hundred fifty years.

Alice Lannon
Michael McCarthy

Open, Open Green House

O nce upon a time in a far away land there lived a beautiful young girl named Maggie. She lived with her father as her mother had passed away when she was very young. They loved each other dearly, and were comfortable and content until her father became quite ill and had to give up working.

Money was scarce, but Maggie helped earn a few pennies by running errands, taking care of the neighbours' children, and selling her embroidered cloths.

Sometimes Maggie would go to bed hungry, saving the meagre rations for her ailing father. She wished she could earn some money so that her father could see a doctor for his illness, and get treatment and medicine to make him well and strong again.

Returning home one evening she heard the town crier calling out the news. He said that once again an anonymous person was offering a bag of gold for anyone who stayed alone for three nights in the haunted castle known as *Green House*.

Maggie had often heard the story of Green House, but she thought nothing about it. She could see it, or at least the top of it, from their own cottage. It was almost covered by forest that had grown up around it, and was green in colour so everyone called it Green House.

As she walked home she could think of nothing else but the bag of gold. She made up her mind she was going to have it, and make her father well again.

Maggie was up early the next morning and at the town office waiting for it to open. When she told the town clerk what she wanted he only laughed at her. "Many a strong man has tried to win that gold, but has failed to stay even one night. Even brave soldiers were scared away," he told her.

Maggie told him why she wanted the money, and when he saw she was serious about it he decided to let her try. He told her to come back in a couple of days and he would give her an answer.

Before she left she asked him if she could take a lunch, also a little dog and a cat to keep her company if she was allowed to stay at Green House.

Two days later her request was granted, and Maggie was so excited fear never entered her mind. She asked a neighbour to check on her father, and she told him she would be away a few nights in connection with work, which wasn't exactly a lie.

Maggie was escorted to the castle just before dark on a cold, wintry evening. She had a bag of apples, some nuts and her little dog and cat with her.

The town clerk seemed nervous as they neared the place, and as soon as they entered the big ballroom he showed her the box of logs which she was to use to keep the fire going; he then hurried away telling her, as he left, to come and see him the next morning at nine if she stayed all night. He felt sure she would return home long before that.

Before Maggie settled down for the night she decided to take a look around the old castle. Going up a winding staircase that creaked and groaned with her every step, the flickering candle cast ghostly shadows on the walls, and huge cobwebs hung from the high ceiling like ropes.

On either side of a wide hall were many doors. As Maggie opened them she could see that once these rooms must have been very beautiful, but now they lay covered with a thick layer of dust, even some of the frills on the bedspreads were beginning to rot away and fall unevenly. She felt sad to think of the much happier times this old house must have known.

Once downstairs she discovered a large room that must have been the dining room. It was filled with rows of long tables and chairs which she thought could seat a hundred for sure. Next to that was a large kitchen and pantry. She felt this old castle had once been a cheery place.

On returning to the room with the fire she put on some more logs, and the flames danced and flared. She noticed that this was the only room that looked like it had been used recently. The floor was clean and shiny and the dancing flames gave it a warm glow. Making herself comfortable, she settled down for what she thought was going to be a long night.

It seemed to her that the wind had picked up and the old loose shutters rattled, and a loose board banged against the side of the house. The wind whistled in the chimneys, and howled mournfully around the corners. She was not afraid, but wondered what had scared off the others who had tried for the bag of gold.

A big old clock ticked loudly, and close to the hour of midnight loud noises were heard outside. There was shrieking and groaning and wailing and the thunderous stamping of feet.

At the stroke of midnight three loud knocks came on the door.

"Who is there?" called Maggie.

A voice asked, "All alone fair maid?"

"All alone I am not, I have my apples to eat, my nuts to crack, my little dog and pussy cat, and all alone I am not."

The little dog began to whine, but Maggie told him not to be afraid, and the cat cuddled closer to her.

A loud voice then called out, "Open, Open Green House and let the king's son in!"

The double door swung open, and in trooped the weirdest looking gang of people Maggie had ever seen. Their faces were like horrible masks, and there must have been a hundred of them. The last to enter were six men carrying a large canvas bag followed by an old witch.

She ordered the men to place the bag on the table and untie the rope. She muttered a magic spell, and there stood a handsome young man dressed like a prince.

Maggie's heart was beating wildly, and as the ugly faces sneered, and scowled at her, she was tempted to get up and run away, but when she thought of her father and how sick he was, her courage was soon restored, and she decided to stick it out.

Then the music started and the ghostly troop began to dance fiercely, wildly, and in a frenzy they dipped and whirled faster and faster.

Maggie felt cold shivers run up her spine as the dancers came closer and closer, making dire threats as they passed her. However, they didn't touch her and she relaxed a little. She noticed that the old witch never changed partners, but danced only with the fine-looking young man. Once as they passed Maggie she noticed the sad expression on his face and how gentle his eyes looked. He seemed to be trying to say something to her, so she watched him more closely.

The next time they passed the old witch's back was turned and the young man looked into Maggie's eyes and mouthed, "Stay for three and I'll be free." Maggie's determination to stay was stronger now, and nothing would make her leave.

The strange party continued until just before daybreak. Then, at a signal from the witch, the music stopped and the wand touched the young man who immediately fell lifeless to the floor. He was placed in the canvas bag which was then tied and hoisted on the shoulders of the men who had brought him in. The howling and the wailing began again as they all trooped out shrieking and screaming, leaving Maggie, her cat and her dog alone.

She heard a cock crow somewhere in the distance, and knew the night had passed. Except for the memory of the look in the young man's eyes it seemed like a nightmare. Looking around her, Maggie decided that they would have to do more than make faces and threats the next night to scare her away, but she wondered what was in store for her as the memory of the handsome young man only made stronger her resolve to earn the bag of gold.

The next morning people gathered in the town's square and the talk was of nothing else but of how Maggie had spent the night in the haunted house. They gathered around her as she came out of the town office all curious to know what happened. She just smiled, told them nothing and hurried home.

Maggie entered the castle the next evening for the second time with mixed emotions. She couldn't get the pleading look of the young man who seemed to be under the witch's spell out of her mind, and she found herself anxiously awaiting the midnight party.

Just before midnight the wind seemed to grow stronger, and the whole castle seemed to shake and rattle as had happened the night before. A loud ruckus was heard outside and the tramping of heavy footsteps came closer. When the clock began to strike twelve three loud knocks came on the door.

Maggie asked who was there. She was greeted with, "All alone fair maid?"

She answered as she had the night before. "All alone I am not, apples to eat and nuts to crack, a little dog and a pussy cat, all alone I am not."

This was followed by the command "Open, Open Green House and let the king's son in!"

The hideous characters trooped in and their sinister faces matched the moaning and groaning they were making. The six men carrying the canvas bag did as before, and the old witch once more muttered her magic spell and the fine young man stood up. Maggie's heart beat wildly, and she couldn't take her eyes off him. The witch saw this and said, "If you want to keep those eyes you'd better keep them to yourself." The piercing look in her fiendish eyes let Maggie know she meant her threat.

The dancing was fast and furious. The music thumped and banged while the ghostly figures almost flew around the room. The wind they made nearly tipped over Maggie's chair so she moved closer to the wall. As they passed the fireplace, the flames seemed to reach out into the room making the smoke from them sting Maggie's eyes making it difficult to see. But when she stole a glance at the prince, he mouthed, "Be brave for me."

Every time the witch passed Maggie she uttered threats trying to make her leave. But Maggie was not a quitter, she had two reasons now to stay—the fate of the handsome prince, as well as the bag of gold to make her father well.

As the night wore on the scare tactics got more vicious, and Maggie was frightened when she heard the witch say she was thinking of throwing her into the fire if she didn't soon leave. Maggie realized these were just threats and decided to stick it out.

Just before daybreak the party came to a stop. Once more the spell was uttered, and the young man was placed back in the sack. When they all left quiet returned. Maggie could see the sky beginning to lighten, so she put another log on the fire, and dozed for a few hours dreaming of the handsome prince.

The next morning the townspeople were waiting for Maggie as she came out of the town's office all curious about what had happened. Maggie told them nothing and some of them muttered among themselves, saying they were fools to believe all those stories that had been told about the big green house on the hill.

As Maggie entered the castle on the third night she was filled with fear and apprehension, knowing that the old witch would try her utmost to scare her away from the castle. Maggie didn't feel like eating tonight. She just cuddled the cat closer, and had the dog lie across her feet which gave her some comfort.

As it neared the hour of midnight the blood curdling noises started again. The shutters banged louder and louder—the castle shook, and the howl of the wind was terrifying as it blew down the fireplace, forcing the flames and smoke into the room as before. Then the uncanny trampling was heard getting louder and louder as it neared the castle. Once again as on the previous nights a loud knocking came on the door, and the usual questions were asked. Maggie answered in a loud clear voice as she had the other two nights. Her voice belied the dread in her heart.

The witch called for the house to open and let the king's son in. The doors burst open and the grim troop lined up by the table, and watched as the young man was brought back to life.

Maggie's heart beat wildly at the sight of him, and she felt a strong attraction for the stranger. As the music started the old witch fixed her evil eye on Maggie, and pointing her bony fingers at the most grisly characters, ordered them to crowd around her, reaching out their taloned-like fingers as if to strike her, but just missing their target. Maggie trembled and felt the urge to run for her life.

Yet in the same instance she could see her father's pale face and her courage returned. She also caught a glimpse of the prince, and this time she saw a glimmer of hope in his eyes.

"Do your worst," she thought, "I'll not leave." The dance became wilder and the hideous creatures came closer, almost smothering her—their foul breath made her qualmish. The night seemed to drag. The old witch, so intent on frightening Maggie, had forgotten about the time, and when the cock crowed everything came to a standstill. The old witch tried to utter her spell but only a sickly groan was heard. She slumped to the floor and shrunk away to nothing, disappearing into a small puff of smoke. The motley crew vanished the same way. All that was left was the handsome young prince who shouted with joy, and took a startled Maggie in his arms.

He told Maggie how the wicked witch had put a spell on him a very long time ago. It took her brave deed of staying in the castle for three nights to break the spell. She told him about her sick father and why she needed the gold.

He asked her to marry him and be his princess of Green House once they had it restored to its original beauty. Maggie agreed to be his wife, and they both went to tell her father the good news. Her father was soon well and strong again, and Maggie and her prince lived happily ever after.

Big Black Bull
of Hollow Tree

nce upon a time there were three sisters, Darling Dinah, Kitty and Marie. These three girls were in their teens and very pretty young ladies they were! Darling Dinah and Marie were very demure and gentle, but Kitty, the youngest, was a bit of a tomboy and bubbled with energy.

The three girls lived with their grandmother in a remote country region where strange tales were told of wicked witches having satanic powers which they sometimes used on innocent victims for no apparent reason. It was also reported that a big black bull was often seen wandering around the forest, but no one knew his owner, and some people whispered that it was actually a prince doomed to live the life of a bull because of an evil witch's curse. He was known by the name of *Big Black Bull of Hollow Tree*.

The three young girls loved to wander through the shady forest, and they took long walks every day. Their grandmother warned them about going to a certain part of the woods, but like all young people this only made them very curious, and one day when they came near the forbidden area, they decided to have a look.

At first they saw only trees and an occasional grassy spot, but on closer inspection they found a fenced-in section. The high board fence hid whatever was inside. They walked around the area looking for a gate, but no gate could be found. Kitty tried to climb the wall but it was no use, and the young ladies were about to give up when they noticed a loose board. Pushing aside the board they were able to squeeze through.

They looked at each other in disappointment. There was nothing to be seen but some trees, a few large stones, and a couple of grassy spots—about the same as outside the fence. As they were about to leave a peculiar shaped rock caught their attention. It was shaped like a big arm chair and completely covered with moss, and upon a closer look they saw some faded letters had been carved into the stone. The curious girls scraped away the moss, and soon the words, *Make a Wish* became visible. The girls were delighted. "A wishing chair," they said, "let's make a wish."

Darling Dinah sat in the chair and said, "I wish a nice young man would come and marry me." Marie was next and her wish was the same as her sister's.

Finally Kitty jumped in the chair and said, "I wish the Big Black Bull of Hollow Tree would come after me." The girls laughed and giggled about their find, and the two older girls hoped their wishes would come true. Kitty gave no thought to her wish as she didn't believe in such silly things as wishing chairs.

The girls hurried home feeling rather guilty about disobeying their grandmother's orders. The grandmother noticed nothing strange about the girls although they were unusually quiet at supper time. After the dishes were washed, and they were sitting around the fire, a loud knock came on the door. The grandmother opened it, and two strange men pushed passed her, and went and stood by Darling Dinah and Marie.

"What is the meaning of this?" asked the grandmother.

"We've come to claim our brides," they answered. The old lady was powerless, and now knew that the girls had found the wishing chair. She consoled herself that at least they were handsome young men and Kitty was not involved.

The weddings were planned for the next night and the men left. The grandmother worried about the fact that she knew nothing of these young men who were going to marry her granddaughters. Because they came in answer to a wish made in the *wishing chair* worried her more.

The next night the marriages took place in the village church, and a small reception was held at the home of the brides. Some music and dancing were being enjoyed by the assembled neighbours when a loud noise was heard above the revelry. It sounded like someone was trying to get in. The music stopped and the door was pushed open, and in came a big black bull. Everyone was astonished as the bull headed for Kitty, picked her up on his horns and left. The merriment ceased at Kitty's departure, for the grandmother was sick with grief, and blamed herself for not doing more to keep her granddaughters from the evil wishing chair.

Darling Dinah and Marie were also in for a rude awakening for when they were alone with their husbands they faced a big decision. The question put to them was this. "Do you want a man in the day and a snake in the night, or a man in the night and a snake in the day?"

The two sisters took the "man in the day" choice. The grandmother discovered this, for when passing their rooms she saw a huge snake curled up on each of their pillows. The two *snakemen* took their brides to their own homes after the wedding night, and whenever the girls visited their grandmother they seemed to be content. Kitty often came to see her grandmother too and always seemed happy. Big Black Bull would bring her on his horns, and Kitty loved the ride through the woods.

The grandmother noticed one day that Kitty was in the family way and she worried more than ever. After that visit it was a long time before Kitty visited again, but she never mentioned the baby. There was a faint look of sadness in Kitty's eyes though, however, she still seemed to be fairly happy. The old grandmother was very curious but she didn't pry, and during the next five years the same thing happened twice more. However, no questions were asked or answered.

On one visit to her grandmother, Kitty and Big Black Bull decided to stay overnight. When the old grandmother heard them snoring she tiptoed into their bedroom and peeped in. There sleeping soundly was a handsome young man with his arms about Kitty. On the floor by the side of the bed lay the hide and horns of a big black bull. Kitty's grandmother crept inside the room, grabbed the horns and hide, dragged it down the stairs and threw it into the fire.

Soon the stench of burning hair wafted through the house. All of a sudden the young man jumped out of Kitty's bed, groaning as if in great pain and pulled on his pants and shirt. In his hurry he struck his nose on the bedpost, and three drops of blood fell on his white shirt. He ran down the stairs and out the door as if the Devil was at his heels. Kitty ran after him for a couple of minutes, then when she saw he was going in the opposite direction of their home, she returned to her grandmother's house, dressed herself and set out in pursuit of her husband.

Kitty called out to him, but in vain, he didn't even look back, and he seemed to be doubling the space between them. As she went up one hill he was going down another. The road was rough and rocky, and poor Kitty became so tired she felt she couldn't go any further. On seeing a light she decided to seek shelter for the night.

Her knock was answered by a kind young woman about her own age. She welcomed Kitty and gave her food and a bed for the night. She had three children, and Kitty noticed that a little boy was about the same age as her first born. Kitty often wondered where her children were, and when she would see them, for when they were born they were taken away to a secret place, so that the wicked witch who had put the spell on Big Black Bull could not harm them. He promised Kitty that soon the spell would be broken, and then they would all live happily together. Kitty had been living in hope that this would soon come to pass, but what would happen now?

Before she left the cottage the next morning, the kind lady gave her a little gift to help her in her search. It was a small ball with a string attached, and it had a special power for when tossed ahead of a person it would make the roughest path smooth. Kitty thanked her kindly and set out in pursuit of her husband.

The special ball made the going much easier for Kitty, and she covered many more miles than she had the previous day. Only once did she catch a glimpse of her loved one, and he was far ahead of her. She travelled on until nightfall, and then asked for shelter at the first cottage she came to.

Once again Kitty was made welcome and treated kindly. Here, with other children was a little girl who was very friendly towards her, and when she gave Kitty a kiss and hug, her heart was filled with love and longing for her little girl who would be about the same age as this child.

When Kitty was leaving the next morning the kind hostess gave her a small remembrance of her stay. It was a magic tablecloth. When one was hungry all that was necessary was to spread the cloth and make a wish. The food would appear, ready to eat. Kitty was more than grateful and thanked her kind hostess.

All day Kitty travelled, and this time she found the going much easier. The ball made the rough road smooth and level. A couple of times she thought she saw her husband's white shirt off in the distance, but soon lost sight of him again. She kept on until it got dark, and again sought shelter at the first house she came to.

Once again Kitty was treated kindly, and here a baby about the age of her last baby was sleeping in a crib. Oh, how Kitty longed to hold her own baby in her arms.

The clothes Kitty was wearing began to look the worse for wear. She had left in such a rush that she took nothing but what she had on at the time. When she mentioned this to the lady of the house she was presented with a pair of magic shears as a gift. All she had to do was snip around the torn edges of her clothes and they became like new. Once again Kitty was overcome with emotion at the kindness of strangers. She thanked the lady for her gift and continued on her journey.

Around noon Kitty stopped to rest and eat. She spread her cloth, and made a wish for something cool to eat and drink. Immediately a tall glass of cold lemonade and a large bowl of ice cream was put before her on the magic tablecloth. As she enjoyed her refreshment she could see someone near a brook. When she finished eating she decided to ask if anyone had passed that way.

On arriving at the brook, she noticed that a girl was washing something in it, and crying.

"What is the trouble my dear?" she asked kindly.

Through her sobs the girl answered, "I shall be punished very severely if I can't get the stain out of this shirt."

"Here, let me try," said Kitty and took the shirt in her hands. She knew at once it was her husband's shirt and she rubbed it with soap and then rubbed the material together. The stain at once disappeared.

The young girl was very grateful, and wondered how she could show the stranger her thanks. "You can do that," said Kitty, "by telling me how to find the man who was wearing this shirt."

"Over the hill there is a house where I work for a very mean mistress. I think the owner of this shirt is her prisoner, as my mistress has locked him away in a back room since he arrived yesterday."

Kitty went home with the girl, and asked if she could talk with the man in the back room. At first the old woman made an excuse that the man was too sick to see anyone. However, Kitty offered her the magic shears, and the old woman said she could see him that night.

When Kitty went into the back room, she saw that the man was indeed her husband. However, he failed to recognize her as he had been heavily drugged. Kitty sat by his side all night, and every now and then would call out to him, "Oh Big Black Bull of Hollow Tree, three fine babes I bore for thee, and now you won't turn to me."

The second night Kitty had to give the old woman her magic ball to see her husband. Once again he was too doped up to talk, but he smiled at her before falling into a deep sleep.

The next day Kitty got a message to him through the girl when she went to do his room. She told him that she had to talk, and for him to only pretend to drink the glass of milk that the old woman took into him just before she allowed Kitty inside the room. She suggested that he spill the milk under the bed when the old woman wasn't looking.

On the third night Kitty gave her the magic tablecloth. Tonight her husband pretended to be asleep when the old crone brought Kitty in the room. As soon as the old woman left them alone, Kitty fell into his arms and begged to know why he had left so suddenly. He told Kitty that when his bull outfit was destroyed he could not be seen as a man in the day, or the curse would fall on his children.

He told her the old woman was really a wicked witch, and that almost seven years ago the curse had been put on him and his brothers, and in only a few months the spell would have been broken. Since he could no longer be the bull anymore, he had to come to the witch's house to beg her to free him from the curse. However, she would not agree. The only way out was to kill the wicked creature, and this was not an easy thing to do as the only spot where she could be harmed was a black spot on her left breast.

Every night the old witch rubbed oil on this spot just at the stroke of midnight. A few minutes before twelve o'clock Kitty crept out to the kitchen—sure enough there was the old witch taking off her clothes in the chimney corner. Armed with a sharp-pointed knife, Kitty waited, and just as the old hand dipped in the warm oil, Kitty threw the knife. Right on the black spot it struck, and the old witch fell down shrivelling up to nothing except for a small bit of dust.

At that very moment the *snakemen* married to her sisters awoke in the shape of men to the great delight of their wives.

Kitty and her prince returned home, but not before picking up their three children. They were the children whom Kitty saw when she spent the night at the homes of her three sisters-in-law. The prince had kept their whereabouts a secret for fear the old witch might harm them.

A big family reunion was held, and Darling Dinah, Marie and Kitty all went to live in the big castle with their husbands who ruled wisely over the land, had many children and lived happily ever after.

Jack, Bill and Tom and the Ship that Could Sail Over Land and Water

nce there was an old woman who had three sons—Jack, Bill and Tom. Times were hard, and the poor family had a tough time trying to keep body and soul together.

One night as they sat by the fire talking over their sad plight the mother said that Tom, being the eldest, should leave home to look for work. Tom and Bill were lazy boys, and their mother often warned them that if they didn't change their ways they would surely come to a bad end, and she often wished they were more like their younger brother, Jack.

It was decided that night that Tom would set out the next day to "seek his fortune." Before going to bed, Tom turned to his mother and said, "Bake me a cake in the ashes before the crow flies over the house."

The mother got up in the cold, grey light of dawn and did as she was bid. When the cake was baked she called Tom saying, "Tom, Tom, the cake is ready." As Tom ate his bowl of gruel without sugar or milk he grumbled about not having enough to fill him. The mother showed him the cake and asked, "Will you have the whole of it with my curse, or the half of it with my blessing?"

"The whole of it with your curse is little enough for me," he answered. He pushed the cake into his lunch bag, and hurried out the door without as much as a thank-you or good-bye.

Tom travelled all morning and at noon he came to a nice grassy spot by the side of a river and decided to rest and eat his lunch. When he had eaten a few mouthfuls a funny looking little old man came out of the woods and asked if he might pick up the crumbs as they fell to the ground.

"I'll give you a kick that will land you on the other side of the river," Tom answered. The little old man went sadly away and sat near the edge of the water.

When Tom had finished eating he went to the river to get a drink, but just as he was about to put his mouth in the water the little old man stirred the water with a funny looking stick, and the water turned to blood. This maddened Tom and he made a swipe at the old fellow, but he hopped quickly away singing, "Head on a spear, head on a spear."

Tom continued his journey and before nightfall he came to a big house and grounds. Over the gate was a sign, *Man Wanted.* Tom decided to try his luck so he went to the door. An ugly giant opened it and pulled Tom inside. The old giant looked so ferocious that Tom shivered in his shoes.

"If you want to work for me," the giant said, "you can sleep in the barn, and tomorrow I want that big meadow mowed, before noon too."

Poor Tom was too frightened to ask about food although he was feeling very hungry. It seemed he had just shut his eyes when he was awakened by the angry shouting of the giant, "Get out and mow, I don't pay a man to sleep."

Once again Tom was afraid to ask for breakfast, and found himself so weak from hunger that he could hardly stand, yet his fear gave him strength, and he worked like he never worked before.

Just before noon, Tom was almost finished mowing the meadow, but he felt so weak he had to rest for a moment. He had just sat down when the angry giant came striding towards him with his assistant. He grabbed Tom and lifted him to his feet saying, "I pay for work not for sitting down on the job." He passed Tom to his helper. "Cut off his head and put it on a spear for all to see the results of laziness." Tom had come to a bad end and the old man's prediction had come to pass. The old giant went away chuckling to himself about getting his work done for nothing.

Back home Tom's mother and brothers wondered what had happened to him. Some time passed with no word, so Bill said he would go and try to find out what had become of his brother. He asked his mother to "bake a cake in the ashes before the crow flies over the house" as she had done for Tom.

When the cake was ready his mother called Bill, and while he was eating his meagre breakfast she asked the same question as she had of Tom. "Will you take the half of it with my blessing, or the whole of it with my curse?"

"The whole of it is not enough for me," he answered, and putting the cake in his bundle went off in a great hurry. The poor mother watched him until he was out of sight and wiped the tears from her eyes. She loved her sons dearly and hated them to have to leave home.

Bill followed the same path through the woods that Tom had taken when setting out on his journey. At noon, Bill found the same clearing near the river where Tom had eaten his lunch, and decided it was a good spot to rest and eat.

Bill had just taken a few bites when the little old man came to where he sat and asked for a small morsel. Bill, like his brother, would not share his cake, and threatened to beat up the old man for bothering him. The old man muttered, "Head on a spear," and went and sat by the water's edge. When Bill tried to get a drink the old man stirred the water with his stick, and as before the water was turned to blood. Bill became very angry and chased after him but he vanished calling out, "Head on a spear," before Bill could catch him.

Just before dark Bill came to the giant's house; the sign still said *Man Wanted*, so Bill boldly walked to the door and asked for work. The gruff manner of the giant frightened Bill, and like Tom, he was very hungry. The giant told him to sleep in the barn, and the next morning to go to the field and cut and bundle the corn into sheaves. He warned Bill to have that work finished before noon, or his head would go on the spear.

Bill was awakened at daylight by the giant and told to go to work. When Bill asked for breakfast the giant roared, "Work first, eat after!"

Poor Bill worked without stopping, but just a few minutes before twelve he felt so faint from hunger that he was forced to rest for a moment. The giant was right there to pounce on him, and he grabbed Bill and yelled to his assistant, "Take care of this lazy fellow." Poor Bill joined Tom with his head on a spear.

Six months passed, and Jack and his mother had no word from Bill and Tom, so Jack decided it was his turn to go and seek his fortune.

His mother hated to see Jack leave home. He was kind and thoughtful and a good worker. As he was leaving the house, she asked the same question she had asked the other two boys. "Here's your cake, will you take the whole of it with my curse, or the half of it with my blessing?"

"Oh mother," Jack said, "the half of it with your blessing. Besides I'd like for you to have some for yourself."

"Oh no Jack," she said, "you take it all. I was just testing you." She gave him a big hug and a kiss, and sent him on his way.

Near noon, Jack came to the same grassy spot where his brothers had eaten. As Jack opened his lunchbag he saw a little old man near the edge of the woods. He beckoned for the old man to join him. Jack offered to share his cake with him, and the old man was delighted, and talked of all the wonders he had seen and many things to come. He took from his pocket a bottle of fine wine which he shared with Jack, and made the break a very enjoyable one for both of them.

Jack told the old man he was looking for some news of his brothers and that he was off to seek his fortune. The old man wished him luck, and before he left said, "When you come this way again I'll make a nice surprise for you. I'll build you a ship that can sail over land and water." Jack thought the old man was a little senile, but he thanked him and promised to return before too long.

As Jack reached the place where his two brothers met their sad fate, he saw two dry skulls on spears above the entrance to the grounds. A large sign above the gate said *Man Wanted*. Jack knocked and the giant answered the door and growled, "What do you want?" "Good evening sir," said Jack. "I am here because of your sign, and I am looking for work."

The giant sized him up and said, "Anyone who works for me will not get away with laziness, and if caught his head will be cut off and put on a spear."

"Is that what happened to those two fellows back by the gate?" asked Jack.

"Yes," said the giant, "a fellow called Tom, another called Bill. I caught them sitting down on the job."

Jack now knew the fate of his two brothers and promised to avenge their deaths. But right now he needed work, and asked the giant about the pay, and if board and lodging were included.

The giant thought, "Here's a smart lad, I'll have to be careful with him." He told Jack to sleep on a cot in the back room. Jack not being afraid of the giant said he was hungry, and with that the giant called his cook to feed him.

Jack ate a hearty supper and went to bed. He awoke early and washed and went to the kitchen for breakfast. The old giant noticed this, and said nothing except to tell him that he wanted a large pile of wood cut into logs for his fireplace.

Jack worked without stopping until noon, then he went to the house for lunch, but found the doors locked. No one answered his knock so Jack went back to the woodpile, took a large bundle, and went across the street to a market-place and sold it for some bread, cheese and milk. He was eating his lunch when the angry giant came yelling at him.

Jack stood his ground and said, "You said my food was included in my pay, so when no lunch was available at your house I did something about it. A man can't work on an empty stomach."

Almost a month had passed since Jack had come to work and payday was drawing near. The old giant could find no fault with him, but he was not going to part with his money, and racked his brains for a way to get rid of Jack. He finally thought of a plan to torment an old enemy, and get Jack killed at the same time.

The land next to where Jack worked belonged to an even more ferocious giant who hated people on sight. Jack didn't know this, and just followed orders when he was told to drive his master's herd to pasture in the adjoining meadow.

As Jack was driving the cows along he saw an old woman with a heavy bundle and offered to carry it for her. When she reached her cottage, she made him take a small amount of newly made cottage cheese in return for his kindness. Jack wasn't hungry so he put the cheese in his pocket, thanked her and went on his way.

Jack wondered why the tall grass in the pasture wasn't cut for hay. He didn't have long to wonder for he had just turned the last cow through the gate when he heard the angry shouts of the owner as he came towards him.

"What's a little pipsqueak like you doing on my land, and with my cows as well?"

Jack stood up to the huge giant, and told him that he had orders to bring the herd to this pasture by his master, the giant who lived nearby.

"Well now, my lad, we shall see who is the smartest and strongest of the two of us. We shall have a little contest and the winner takes all. If I win, and win I will, you lose your head and the cattle are mine. If you beat me you take everything I own, castle, lands and all.

Jack had no choice but to go along with the giant. Thinking quickly he put his hand in his pocket and took some of the cottage cheese. He then stooped down, and pretended to pick up a handful of stones, saying as he did so, "Can you squeeze water from those little white stones there on the ground?" As he spoke he squeezed the cottage cheese and the whey ran to the ground.

The giant grabbed a handful of stones and squeezed with all his might, but not one drop of water came out, and the stones turned to dust in his hands. He tried handful after handful and ground them to powder. He ran around in a frenzy grinding up fistfuls of stones until he was covered with dust, and finally gave up in despair.

"Alright, you won that. Now, let's try something else. Come into my house, and we shall see who can drink the most soup.

I have a large pot ready and I'm starving."

Jack thought quickly, and while the old giant washed nearby, splashing water over his face, Jack slipped a soft leather bag out of his pocket and pushed it inside his shirt. After taking his turn at the pump he followed the giant into the kitchen.

The huge pot was filled with good-tasting soup. There was enough to feed an army. The giant ladled out the soup into large bowls, and for each bowl he made a tally mark, scratching it on the table in front of him with a long sharp knife.

The giant drank his soup with gusto and loud noise. So engrossed was he with the job at hand that he didn't see Jack pour the soup down his neck into the leather bag. Jack's stomach seemed to bulge, and the giant was amazed at his capacity. As the last bowl was being drunk Jack had no difficulty in drinking his and the giant was almost too full to get down another spoonful, but he forced it down and then counted the tally marks. He found they were exactly the same.

Jack knew that he was dealing with a sly and cunning rogue, and must think quickly to save himself. He saw the sharp knife on the table near him and had an idea. He said to the giant, "Let me have that knife, and come outside, and I'll show you a good trick." The giant handed Jack the knife and followed him outdoors.

Outside, Jack plunged the sharp knife into the leather bag inside his shirt, and the soup ran down to the ground. The old giant was enraged, "You'll not beat me this time," he roared, and grabbed the knife and plunged it into his stomach. He reeled, staggered and fell forward into a pool of blood and soup.

Jack was now owner of a castle and lands, but his brothers had not been avenged. He still had his master to deal with. He returned with the herd just before suppertime to his master's surprise. When Jack told him he had killed the other ogre, the giant became frightened of Jack, thinking he had some strange powers, and he pleaded for his life. He gave back all the land and also his castle to the farmer from whom he had swindled it in the first place. He gave Jack a big bag of gold for his work, and then left immediately with his servants for a remote region of the world where he lived a solitary life in fear and remorse.

Jack decided he would first take some gold to his mother and then go to seek his fortune. His mother was overjoyed to see her son, but saddened to hear of the fate of Tom and Bill—of course Jack spared her the gory details.

It was with a light heart that Jack set out the second time. He followed the same trail as before, and at noon sat down in the same place as he had the first time.

The little old man welcomed him, and pointing to a pile of sticks, canvas and wire said, "I'm ready to build you a ship that will sail over land and water."

Jack thought the little old man was senile, and went along with the idea so as not to hurt his feelings. He sat on the grass, and watched as the funny looking man went to work, and before Jack's eyes an odd looking shape began to take form.

It was sort of a long hollow box, pointed at the front, and tapered to a tail end with a wind-jack as rudder. On either side was an extension which resembled arms or wings. These were covered with canvas. Near the front was a bench on which to sit while at the helm which was in easy reach, and this controlled the direction in which the ship would move. Behind the bench was a fairly large hold which could be also used as living quarters.

A couple of hours had passed, but it seemed only minutes to Jack who was so taken up with the strange object taking shape before his eyes. Then, the old man invited Jack to come aboard and try her out.

He obeyed, but couldn't believe it when he found the ship lifting off the ground, and had to pinch himself to see if he was dreaming or not as he looked at the trees far below. The old man showed Jack the things he had to do to make sure the ship would go where he wanted. He soon got the knack of it, and was able to steer and guide the ship, and to land and take off again. The old man informed Jack that with this ship he could go any place he wanted, and also told him where he might win a princess for a bride.

In a far-off kingdom there was a beautiful princess who was just of marrying age. This beautiful girl won the hearts of all who met her, but her father promised her hand in marriage only to the one who met certain tasks he set down. So far no one could do what he asked. He told Jack that with his ship, and a crew he might be the one to win the princess.

As Jack was leaving, the old man said that he should pick up the first eight men he saw along the way. He told him to lower down a big bucket and pick up the crew, and when he had eight good men to fly to the far-off kingdom, and try to win the princess for his bride. He wished him luck and sent him on his way.

Jack hadn't gone far when he noticed a man standing by the roadside. He lowered the bucket and motioned for the man to come aboard. The man did not seem a bit surprised to be aboard a ship sailing over land and water.

"My name is Jack, and I'm looking for men to make up my crew. What is your name, and will you work for me?" asked Jack.

"My name is *Run-Fast*, and I'm looking for work. I can do anything a good strong man can do, and I can run faster than anyone else in the world," answered the stranger.

"You'll do fine," said Jack. He continued on his way, and soon another man was seen sitting by the road near a small village. The bucket was lowered again, and this time the man said his name was *Hear-All*, and that he could do anything a good strong man could do, and he could hear things happening on the other side of the world. "You're hired," said Jack.

The next man to come aboard was called, *Never-Be-Warm*, and he was equal to any good strong man at work, but could never get warm enough to suit him.

The fourth man to be taken aboard was *Tear-All*, he too could do a man's work, and could tear anything apart with his bare hands.

The fifth man was called *Hard-Ass*, and could level hills and mountains by just sliding down them. "You'll be very useful," said Jack, and hired him on.

The last three men were *Drink-All*, *See-All*, and *Shoot-All*. Drink-All could drink for days without getting drunk or even feeling good. See-All and Shoot-All worked as a team with See-All pointing out the target, and Shoot-All pulling the trigger.

Jack had chosen his crew, and left to try his luck for the beautiful princess. He was worried and anxious for many men had tried and failed to meet the requirements of the king.

On his way to the palace, Jack saw the princess sitting near the window, and vowed he would never rest until she was his bride. His heart was full of hope and determination as he was taken before the king. Back at the ship the crew waited, and on their master's return noticed how downcast he looked.

"What happened?" they all asked together.

"Tell us, dear master, and we might be of some help," they cried.

"Well, he wants me to send a messenger around the world with a letter, and bring back an answer before nightfall."

"Don't worry, master," said Run-Fast, "I'll go and return early in the afternoon. My legs need stretching and this is a real pleasure for me."

At daybreak Jack and Run-Fast were at the palace gate. The guard gave the runner the sealed envelope and off he started. Jack returned to the ship to await the return of Run-Fast.

At three o'clock there was no sign of the messenger, and Jack was beginning to lose heart. His crew were becoming restless and worried too. They all went up to a big hill to see if he might be on the way, but he was not in sight, and they knew that something must have happened to him. Hear-All put his ear to the ground and said Run-Fast had fallen asleep because he could hear him snoring.

See-All climbed a tall tree and said he could see where Run-Fast was lying on the ground with a *sleepy-pin* in his ear. Shoot-All climbed the tree and aimed his gun where See-All directed. He pulled the trigger, and the pin fell to the ground. Up jumped Run-Fast, and before anyone could thank the two for their good work he was past them, and on his way to the palace with the answer the king had requested.

Later Run-Fast told Jack and the crew how a wicked witch had fooled him by pretending to need help in putting a bundle on her back. When he stooped down to lift the bundle she had slipped the sleepy-pin in his ear.

The king seemed surprised to receive an answer from his letter but to Jack's dismay he said, "You have only passed the first test, now, here is the next one."

He took Jack to his wine cellar which was filled with cask upon cask of fine wines. "I want one man to go into the wine cellar at dusk, and at daylight all these casks must be empty. He must also consume all the wine without getting drunk." Jack said he would talk to his crew, and get back to the king before the fall of night.

When Jack told the crew about the strange request, Drink-All gave a shout of delight. "Hooray! I'll do this for you." But Jack had his doubts.

Guards were placed around the cellar and Jack left Drink-All to try his luck. Jack tossed and turned all night, dreaming of the beautiful princess. He arose early and went to the palace to await the king's order to accompany him to the wine cellar.

Just at daybreak the king and Jack went down the cellar steps. To their amazement Drink-All showed no signs of intoxication and was draining the last few drops from each cask. When he saw Jack he said, "I thought that for once I would get enough to make me feel good, but that was only a taste."

Jack was beginning to get his hopes up when once more a damper was thrown on his spirits. The king said, "The next test involves that hill up there. I want all those trees cleared off, placed in a big pile and burned. A man must stand in the middle of the blaze while the trees are burning. Then I want that hill levelled to a smooth stretch of land. This job must be finished in two days."

With a heavy heart Jack reported back to his crew. "Never fear master," said Tear-All, "these trees will be a bit of fun for me."

Never-Be-Warm grinned and said, "Maybe this time I'll get a little warm, I'm always so cold."

Hard-Ass jumped for joy and cried, "Finally I get to use my skill. That hill will be like child's play for me."

The next morning a large crowd gathered to watch as news spread of the strange feats being performed by the men aboard the ship that could sail over land and water. Jack and the king watched in awe as Tear-All went about his task. Huge trees were pulled from the ground roots and all as if they were matchsticks. Soon the hill was cleared, and a huge pile of trees were thrown to the meadow below. The king gave orders to wait for nightfall to set the fire, and the crowds waited to see Never-Be-Warm do what he claimed he could.

Jack and his crew watched Never-Be-Warm climb to the top of the pile, and burrow a hole in the middle, and sink out of sight. The crowd held its breath as the torch was set to some dry branches at the base of the heap. The flames soon reached the top, and the people wondered if the roar of the fire drowned out the cries of Never-Be-Warm; however, from time to time he could be seen through the flames looking quite contented.

The huge bonfire lasted all night, and at daybreak Never-Be-Warm could be seen raking the glowing coals with his fingers and pulling them close to him in order to get the last bit of warmth from the hot cinders. When he stepped from the ashes he muttered to himself, "Gosh for once I thought I would be really warm but at least I wasn't cold."

No one had to tell Hard-Ass that it was finally his turn. Up the hill he ran and took a running jump, he landed on his bottom and slid down the hill. With him came tons of rock and rubble. He pushed himself along at the foot of the hill spreading the debris to fill the hollows around. He sang and hollered happily as he levelled the big hill to a lovely stretch of smooth earth as far as the eye could see.

Jack had complied with all the king's requests, and now went to the castle to claim his bride. How happy she was to see him for of all the men who had come seeking her hand in marriage he was the only one she really cared for. They had both fallen in love with each other at first sight.

A big wedding was held at the palace and the feats of Jack's crew were told loud and long. The king felt Jack was a worthy man and he piled his riches upon him.

After the wedding Jack took his bride back to the castle he had won from the wicked giant, and there they lived happily ,and had a large family of girls and boys.

Jack's mother came to live with them as did the wonderful crew. They travelled all over the world in the ship that could sail over land and water. No one ever saw the greedy giant or the little old man again.

SECTION TWO

Fairy Lore

THE LITTLE PEOPLE

he early settlers of Newfoundland brought with them from England, Ireland, Scotland and France their traditional oral folklore heritage. Included among many other things was a strong belief in the existence of the *Fairies* or *Little People* — a tiny race of supernatural beings in human form who lived in the woods and rocks near the settlements. They were unpredictable in their relationships with humans and were capable of helping or hurting them.

This belief in the Fairies or Little People was very strong in all parts of Newfoundland, but especially so in areas with a strong Irish or Breton background, and was still pretty general even in the first half of the twentieth century.

Green was the colour of the Fairies, although they usually wore red hats when dancing. It was not safe for humans to wear green clothing for this put them in the power of the Fairies. If you wore green they could command, and you had to do their bidding. This is why green was considered such an unlucky colour in Newfoundland. In fact many Newfoundlanders of the time firmly believed that the St. John's fire of 1892, followed by the Bank Crash of 1894, were caused because in each year the Newfoundland government issued green postage stamps, and so aroused the ire of the Little People.

Tradition has it that the Little People didn't like being called Fairies, and would do something spiteful if they heard you using that name. So, as a safety precaution they were generally referred to as the *Good People* or the Little People.

These Little People, according to an old Newfoundland tradition—that probably came from Ireland with the first Irish settlers—were the angels who stayed neutral in the great Celestial Battle when the Archangel Michael fought Lucifer for control of heaven.

When St. Michael won and Lucifer was cast down into Hell, the question arose of what to do with those angels who had remained neutral. As they had not supported Lucifer they couldn't be sent to Hell, but neither could they remain in Heaven, so they were banished to Earth.

However, although exiled from Heaven they still retained much of their supernatural power, and could work both good and evil on the humans with whom they had to share the Earth.

It was a general belief that the *fairy kingdom* was a beautiful, but enchanted place in a middle kingdom below the surface of the Earth. It was ruled by a king and a queen, and dancing and feasting were the order of the day.

There are many stories of encounters with the Little People in the oral folklore of Newfoundland, and in days gone by few people would travel over long stretches of lonely woods or bogs without taking some precautions against the power of the Fairies.

The main protection was to carry a bit of bread in your pocket, as this would keep the Fairies from having any power over you. In most Newfoundland communities no youngster was ever allowed to go berry picking or trouting without having a bit of bread somewhere about their person. There were also many adults who would never go into the woods alone for fear of being carried away by the Fairies.

If you did come upon Fairies unexpectedly then you had to keep absolutely silent, and give no sign of having seen them. If you showed by word or deed that you had seen them, then you could be *fairy struck*, which meant you fell under their power for certain set periods of time. If, however, you didn't eat in the *fairy kingdom* while a captive then you had to be returned to the world of mortals.

If night overtook you, or you lost your way, and you had no bread on your person, you could protect yourself from the Fairies by turning your coat or jacked inside out. Even the turning out of the pockets of your pants or coat would give you some protection. Despite these safeguards however, there are any number of local stories of persons having come in contact with them. In some cases these persons became *fairy struck* and were never quite right again after these encounters.

In his book *The Path to Yesterday*, John M. Byrnes mentions one well-known Newfoundland character who was supposed to have been "fairied away". This was a man named Stuart Taylor. He lived in St. John's around the turn of the century and was known locally as the *fairy man*. He spent his time constantly playing tunes on a tin whistle that he was supposed to have learned from the Fairies during his stay among them.

In many Newfoundland communities there are old tunes that people say came from the Fairies.

Babies were especially vulnerable to the Little People who were often blamed for switching fairy babies for human ones. The switched baby was called a *changling*. The switch was most likely to be done if the baby was left alone in the house while the mother was hanging clothes outside, or getting a few chips to start a fire. It could also happen when a baby was being carried outside the house. Again, a piece of bread kept in the cradle or carrying bag was the guarantee of safety for the little ones.

One way that you could usually tell if your baby had been switched with a fairy baby was a change for the worst in its features and disposition. If a pretty baby suddenly looked old and all shrivelled up, or a quiet, well behaved baby became unusually cross and cranky, and constantly threw up its milk then it was more than likely a switch had been made. There was, however, a way to get your own baby back again.

To force the Little People to return your child, and take back the changling they had substituted, you had to resort to a desperate cure. It was to take a coal shovel, put it in the fire and keep it there, until it glowed red. Then while announcing in a loud voice that you had had enough and were now going to put the cranky baby on the hot shovel, you went and lifted the child from its crib. You took your time lifting the baby in order to give the Fairies time to switch the babies back again.

In some areas of Newfoundland, people would not talk to strangers about the Little People for fear they might be harmed by them. In his book *Newfoundland Holiday*, J. Harry Smith notes that he was told the people on the Southern Shore believed in Fairies, but when he visited the area not a person would talk about them. Whenever Smith mentioned Fairies there was a dead silence and someone quickly changed the conversation to another topic.

Today the great body of Newfoundland fairy lore has disappeared. No longer do people tell of coming suddenly upon a group of Little People dancing in their circles, nor do children and woodsmen carry a piece of bread to ward off the Fairies. They have been replaced by the more modern mythology of flying saucers, manned by aliens from far distant planets. Like the Little People though, these aliens seem to have a great interest in the affairs of humans.

THE FAIRY THORN

One fine summer's day in the year 1870, a young man from Lawn, Placentia Bay, was making his way home after a visit to the neighbouring town of St. Lawrence. He was about half-way home when he decided to see if the bakeapples were ripe. Leaving the road he walked up a small hill to check out a marsh some distance away. As he crested the hill he saw below him a fairy circle in the marsh, and there were the Little People, all decked out in their green robes and red hats, dancing round and round the circle as fast as their little legs could carry them.

The young man from Lawn had often been warned by his family that if you unexpectedly came up on the Little People dancing you stayed perfectly quiet, and pretended you hadn't seen them as you stole quietly away. If you spoke or in any way showed that you had seen them, then they could harm you.

However, the unexpected sight of the dancers drove the words of warning from the young man's mind, and he clapped his hands and yelled, "Well done!" It was a great mistake as he soon found to his sorrow. At the sound of his voice the dancing stopped and all the Little People glared at him angrily. Then, an old one who seemed to be the leader took something from the pocket of his green robe, and threw it at the gaping stranger.

He felt a sudden jab of pain in his knee and looked down to see what had caused it, but saw nothing. When he lifted his eyes all the Little People had disappeared. His knee began to ache and throb, and he started to make his way back to the road. He made it home, but his knee swelled up and the pain was almost unbearable. He didn't tell his family about his encounter with the Little People because he had forgotten their warnings and made his presence known.

The knee became so swollen and sore that he went to see a doctor at St. Pierre, but the doctor could find nothing to cause the swelling, and none of the medicine he gave did anything to reduce the young man's discomfort.

It was after the visit to the doctor that he confessed about his unexpected encounter with the Little People, and how the leader had thrown something at him. His family then knew it was a *fairy hurt* and no human medicine could help. He would have to suffer until the Fairies took away the pain.

All through winter and spring the young man suffered. Exactly on the first anniversary of his encounter, a small thorn worked its way out of his knee, and almost immediately the knee began to heal.

Needless to say the young man now had a healthy respect for the Little People, and whenever their existence was questioned, the *fairy thorn* was produced as proof of what they could do to humans who broke the strict code of conduct with the fairies.

THE FAIRY CAPTIVE

any years ago in the early nineteenth century, a young man from a small Conception Bay community disappeared while crossing the barrens on a visit to a neighbouring village. When he didn't return by nightfall, and another traveller reported that he hadn't reached his intended destination, a search party was organized. They made a search of the area—not a trace of the missing traveller could be found.

Exactly seven days after his disappearance the missing man returned with a strange story to tell. He told his friends and relatives he had been kidnapped by the Little People, and held captive in their underground kingdom.

He had been about half-way across the barrens when he stopped by a small brook to take a rest. Being a warm day he took off his coat. This was his undoing for underneath the coat he was wearing a bright green sweater.

He was smoking a cigarette when suddenly he found himself surrounded by a large group of tiny people less than a foot high. They were all dressed in bright green, and wore funny little bright red hats all decorated with little feathers. They danced around him pointing to his green sweater and chanting a strange song.

The traveller then made his second mistake, he sat up and asked what they were doing.

"Welcoming you to the kingdom of the Little People," said one of them who wore a kind of crown, and seemed to be their leader.

The traveller protested that he had no intention of joining them, but the dancers all pointed to his green sweater, and the leader asked why he came to the fairy dancing place wearing their colour if he didn't intend to join them. The young man tried to explain that he didn't know the place where he stopped to rest was one of their dancing places, and wearing green in the world of mortals didn't have anything to do with wanting to join the Little People.

They didn't believe him, and since he wore their colour and had spoken to them he was totally in their power. Despite his protests they led him away by a secret path to their underground kingdom. Here he was seated on a stone, and they began to work on persuading him to join them.

First, a beautiful young woman came to him, singing and playing sweet music, and trying to persuade him to become one of them. Suspecting that if he said yes to this beautiful fairy maiden he could never return to the world of the mortals. He refused, and then the Little People became very very angry. He was stripped of his clothes and chained to the stone on which he had been seated. Then, the whole population of Little People pelted him with mud and rocks. To prove that he had been chained the traveller showed his ankles and wrists where the chain marks were still clearly visible.

After being showered with stones, he was punished by having water flung in his face by a gang of small fairy urchins. He endured the punishments as best he could. Then the leader came again and threatened him with terrible punishments if he didn't agree to join them. He still refused. So, he was left chained to the rock. All night he remained in chains and in the morning they brought him food. He was nearly dying of hunger, and reached out his hand to take some bread when an especially ugly looking little man whispered in his ear, "Don't eat it. I was a mortal like you once, but I ate their bread and can never go back to the land of mortals."

The traveller refused to eat, and for a whole week, he was kept chained to the rock and subjected to torments, mocked and made fun of. He began to grow faint from lack of nourishment.

At the end of a week's stay the leader of the Little People ordered that he be flogged with fairy switches for daring to wear their colour, and then returned to the world of the mortals.

The whipping was carried out with whips of thorny bushes, and he nearly died of pain and agony. In proof of what he was saying, the man pulled up his shirt and showed his back all covered with small scratches and bruises. When the whipping was finished, a fairy barber shaved him, and he was thrown into a nearby stream. His clothing was returned, and he was led back to the place where he had been kidnapped.

The man slowly recovered from his ordeal. The bruises and scratches on his back healed over, but he carried the scars of the fairy whipping until his death. He also remembered some of the strange music he had heard while among the Little People and sometimes would play the sweet haunting melodies that he had heard in fairyland.

SECTION THREE

Miracles, Prophecy and Witchcraft

How the Devil Came to Red Island

Today, Red Island, Placentia Bay is uninhabited—just one of the many communities that disappeared during the Smallwood Resettlement Program. However, for more than two centuries Red Island was a vibrant Placentia Bay fishing community with its own unique body of local history, recorded both in song and story.

Among the stories passed down from one generation of Red Islanders to another was the legend of how a rock on one of the highest peaks overlooking the community came to have the imprint of a cloven hoof.

The incident leading up to this curious imprint happened sometime during the early days of the nineteenth century. This was a time when Red Island was an important stopover for fishing schooners taking on bait for a new voyage to the Grand Banks.

It was a night late in spring and the harbour of Red Island was filled with banking schooners, which meant there were a lot of strangers about. At one house, where the owner had a small shop set up in a back kitchen, a game of six-handed auction was in progress. At ten thirty, although the game wasn't finished, one of the players was called back aboard his ship. His partner, a local man, was very annoyed at this for they were close to winning the game. He threw down his cards in disgust saying, "I'd take the Devil for my partner now, if he was available."

The other players only laughed and said they would have to start over again with five-handed railroad auction. At that moment a stranger entered the shop, and the owner of the house went to serve him. The stranger bought some tobacco, and seeing the card players in the other room hoped they were having good luck with the game.

"I was," said the man who had lost his partner, "but 'tis gone now that my partner had to go back on board." The thought struck him that perhaps the stranger might take over the other man's place. He put out a tentative feeler. "I don't suppose you play auction yourself now?"

"Indeed I do," smiled the stranger. "It's one of my favourite games."

"Well then," said the owner of the house, "why don't you join us for a few hands?"

"Nothing would please me more," said the stranger and came forward. However, as he passed from the shop to the house he seemed to trip on the door threshold, and was falling backwards when the owner of the house caught him and helped him over it. He thanked the man and took the seat the other player had just vacated.

The game began again and the stranger's partner was delighted. Every time they bid, whether it was twenty, thirty for sixty, or slam-bang, they got the cards they needed and won everytime.

Game after game it was the same thing, the smiling stranger and his partner were unbeatable. The stranger almost seemed to be able to read his partner's mind.

Then, the unexpected happened. The stranger's partner dropped a card under the table and bent down to get it. He got the shock of his life, for right across from him under the table he could see that the stranger had pulled one of his feet from his shiny black leather boot to rest it, but instead of a foot the man could plainly see a cloven hoof.

The words he had uttered earlier came back to him, and he knew that without intending to he had conjured up the Devil from Hell. Although terribly shaken he knew that he must keep calm and get help to deal with his demonic partner.

He picked up his lost card and handed it to the dealer. Then he excused himself saying he had to go outside "to see a man about a dog" and left.

Luckily for him, the parish priest of the area who didn't reside on Red Island was making his spring visitation for Easter duty. The man went to him, confessed what he had said, and begged the priest for help. The good Father put on his stole, took a cross, a bottle of holy water and his breviary, and accompanied his visitor back to the scene of the card game.

They entered and at once the stranger gave a mocking smile, and removing his hat bowed to the priest revealing at the same time a set of small pointed horns that the hat had hidden. There was a gasp of horror from the other card players who up to this time had suspected nothing, and then the priest spoke.

"I see you are here," he said to the Devil, "and up to no good I wager."

"I was invited," the Devil replied calmly, "and helped to my seat."

"Well then, it's time you went," said the priest, and lighting a candle he began to swiftly read Latin prayers. The Devil sat looking amused until the priest suddenly sprinkled him with holy water, and in the name of God ordered him to depart. As the water fell over him, the Devil uttered a scream followed by a torrent of black oaths. In a great burst of fire and brimstone he disappeared through the roof of the dwelling leaving a gaping hole in the roof.

The priest, followed by the card players, rushed outside in time to see the Devil land on the hill overlooking the harbour. He stood there for a moment, shook his fist at the onlookers, and then disappeared in the direction of Merasheen Island.

A few days later it was discovered that the Devil had left the imprint of his cloven hoof in the rock where he had landed.

The hole in the roof of the house where the Devil had played cards was repaired, but on each succeeding anniversary of the Devil's visit, the hole would reappear and have to be redone.

For generations afterwards the story of how the Devil came to a card game at Red Island was told. The imprint of the cloven hoof was shown as proof of the visit. The story has passed into legend and become a part of the folklore of Placentia Bay.

THE BLACK STICK MEN

In the old days on the southwest coast there was a belief that certain men of the area could work the *black stick* to do both good and evil.

The black stick was a short, slender piece of burnt wood that these men always kept on their person. Possession of the black stick bestowed great power on its possessor, including a total command of the elements, and they could always bend the winds and the tides to their will.

In order to gain possession of a black stick it was necessary to enter into a pact with the Devil. In return for their soul delivered at a certain time, they were given the *dark power* which was activated by touching the black stick. It was whispered in the communities where these men lived that once a year, at midnight on New Year's Eve, the *black stick men* had to go to the top of the highest hill in the area, and meet with the Devil to renew their contract or they would immediately be carried off to Hell.

There is a story from the Burin Peninsula about an encounter a highway road crew had with a black stick man back in the early nineteen fifties. It happened while they were building some branch roads to some of the small communities along the Burin Peninsula.

In one of these communities there lived an elderly gentleman who was said to be a black stick man. He had often given clear proof of his power by giving fair winds to travellers from other communities, and doing other favours. Now, as the road came near his home community he wanted a job for his youngest son.

He walked to the highroad camps, about five miles from his home village, and asked to see the boss, Mr. B., who told him he was sorry but there were no jobs available. At that very moment a large bulldozer stopped on the road outside, and the driver ran in to drop off a message at the camp office.

The black stick man took in the scene, and then in a quiet voice said to Mr. B., "Until my son gets a job, that thing out there," and he pointed to the bulldozer, "won't move an inch." At that very moment the dozer's engine went dead.

The old man without further word went out of the camp office, and sat on a stump across the road from the dozer. He took out his pipe, filled it and settled down for a comfortable smoke.

The driver hurried out of the office and back to his machine. He tried to start it but it wouldn't even catch. Again and again he tried but it wouldn't go. He called the maintenance mechanic, who came out and worked on it but had no luck. It just wouldn't start. All this time the black stick man sat and smoked away.

Traffic began to build up both behind and in front of the dozer, but nothing could get by. An hour passed, two, three hours passed, the mechanic still worked away but with no results. The motorist began to grow more than a little impatient.

Then a motorist from the old man's village came, and saw him sitting on the stump. He immediately suspected he had something to do with the hang-up.

"What's he doing here?" he asked one of the road crew.

"Came in looking for a job for his young feller," he replied.

"Did he get one?"

"No," he said, "the boss turned him down."

The motorist immediately went to see Mr. B. and told him what he suspected. Mr. B. only laughed at first, until he realized the other man was serious. Finally, he agreed to go and offer the old man a job for his son if he could get the dozer to start up.

Mr. B. approached the old man who was still sitting on the stump. "If I give your son a job will that infernal machine start?"

"Certainly," said the old man, "I told you that in the office."

"Okay then, he can start work tomorrow morning."

"Thank you, sir," said the old man getting up. "Now tell him," pointing to the driver, "to give her a try."

The driver shrugged his shoulders and climbed back into the cab. He pressed the starter, the machine roared into life, and purred like a kitten.

Needless to say, the black stick man's son had a job for the rest of the construction season.

THE DEVIL'S STAIRCASE

On a high steep headland at the approach to Cape Broyle is seen the *Devil's Staircase*. According to an old Southern Shore legend this headland got its name when the Devil hoisted a pirate ship up the sheer face of the cliff, and perched it on the top of the rocky summit, three hundred feet above the sea. Here the skeleton of the ship remained for several centuries.

It is said to have happened around the first quarter of the seventeenth century when pirates freely cruised the Newfoundland waters, and Cape Broyle harbour was one of their favourite haunts.

A certain pirate whose deed, but not his name has come down to us, became becalmed off the high headland now known as the Devil's Staircase.

He was in a hurry to get to sea to intercept the Spanish treasure fleet which was soon due to cross the Grand Banks but it was dead calm. Growing angrier by the moment the pirate captain tried whistling for a wind but that was to no avail, the sea remained calm. The pirate captain then flew into a rage, and called on the Devil, promising to serve him faithfully forever if he would only make the ship move. The Devil answered his plea and arrived on board the becalmed ship.

After suitable negotiations had been carried out, and everything was signed and sealed the Devil agreed to move the ship. The crew were ordered to stand by to trim the sails, and the captain took the tiller. With a mighty force the Devil kept his promise. He lifted the ship and planked her down hard on the mountaintop, jarring the bones of the terrified sailors, and the ill-fated captain was immediately dragged off to Hell.

The ship remained at the top of the three hundred foot cliff for many years until the elements and the ravages of time reduced it to a pile of dust. The headland crossed into legend as the Devil's Staircase.

The 1819 Witchcraft Trial at St. Mary's

There are many stories of witches and witchcraft in the annals of Newfoundland folklore. However, there is only one case on record where an accusation of witchcraft was actually examined in a Newfoundland courtroom. This took place at a surrogate court at St. Mary's, St. Mary's Bay on October 8, 1819, and it was the accused witch who brought the action against her detractor. The presiding surrogate judge was Mr. N. Glascock, Esq.

The plaintiff, Jane Halleran, appeared before Mr. Glascock and complained that Catherine Walsh of the same community had falsely accused her of practising witchcraft. She prayed that the surrogate, Mr. Glascock, might issue a summons for Catherine Walsh to appear before the court and prove the witchcraft slander she had uttered.

Mr. Glascock agreed to order Catherine Walsh to appear in court to prove her accusations, and a summons was issued for her appearance at the St. Mary's courtroom on October 15, 1819, before the local magistrate, Mr. Phippard.

Mr. Glascock ordered that Mr. Phippard should examine the case closely before rendering any judgement.

Mr. Phippard was in no hurry to proceed with the case, and it wasn't until November 25 of that year that Jane Halleran had her day in court. Despite the fact that she had been served a court summons to appear, Catherine Walsh did not come. The case however, proceeded without her being present.

After being sworn in, the plaintiff told the court that the defendant, Catherine Walsh, had publicly accused her of deliberately going to the nearby community of Peter's River and stopping her cow from giving milk by the force of her witchcraft. The plaintiff had met the defendant at the house of James McGrath her neighbour, and afterwards Catherine Walsh had gone over to Peter's River and repeated her accusation of witchcraft.

Jane Halleran produced two witnesses who had heard the defendant make the accusation of witchcraft against her.

The first witness was Hugh Kelly of St. Mary's. He said under oath that he had heard Catherine Walsh say that she suspected no other person but the plaintiff for the loss of her cow's milk.

The second witness, Ellen Peddle, also of St. Mary's, stated that she had heard the defendant say that she suspected no other person but the plaintiff for stopping her cow from giving milk — but still she could not say that she did.

As the defendant was not in the court, there was no further evidence given, and Magistrate Phippard gave his verdict.

It was a strange verdict because it neither proved nor disproved Catherine Walsh's accusation against Jane Halleran. All the magistrate said was that the case comprised such inconsistencies, and with the defendant not being present, his verdict was that the defendant should pay ten pence, the cost of the summons to the constable serving it.

So ended the only case of alleged witchcraft to make it to the courts of Newfoundland.

THE WITCH'S CURSE

I n the summer of 1915 a triple drowning tragedy oc- curred in Fortune Bay which the people of the area firmly believed was brought about by the curse of a local woman who was believed to practise witchcraft.

The woman, a widow of many years, lived with her blind son in a small Fortune Bay fishing village where she was greatly feared by all her fellow villagers. It had been often seen that her curses never failed to bring ill luck, misery, and even death to those un- fortunate enough to fall under her displeasure.

The triple drowning according to local legend began when the relieving officer of the day received orders from St. John's to cut as many people as possible from the welfare rolls in order to help the Newfoundland war effort.

Now, the blind boy had been receiving a small government pen- sion, but in his wisdom the welfare officer decided that he was one of those to be cut from further government assistance.

Chartering a friend's motor yacht the officer set out to visit all the communities under his jurisdiction to tell the people he had cut from the welfare rolls that they were no longer entitled to wel- fare of any kind.

In due course, he arrived at the community where the widow and her blind son lived, and informed her that her blind son would not be getting any more help from the government. The widow begged and pleaded with him to reconsider his decision but all in vain. There would be no more government assistance for her blind son.

When the officer left the widow's house, and went down to the shore to row back aboard his yacht, the widow with her blind son by the hand followed him, still begging him to reconsider. He didn't bother to answer her, but began to row out to the motor yacht anchored in the harbour.

Then the widow, holding the blind boy by the hand, waded out knee-deep in the water, and lifting her hands over the waves she called down a terrible curse on the government official. Those standing near by knowing and fearing her dark power shuddered as she intoned her curse, "Let the sea take him and those who would help him, and never may their bodies rest in the earth." She then waded back to land and returned to her house. The official boarded his motor yacht, and left the community.

At the same time the lighthouse keeper on St. Jacque's Island was up in the tower cleaning and refueling the light. He had his telescope with him, and once in a while he rested from his labours and looked at the ships moving in the bay. He saw the motor yacht come out of the widow's community and then went back to his work. A little while later he looked down the bay again to see how the yacht was doing, and to his horror saw that it was floating upside down not too far from the widow's village. There was no sign of the two men in the boat. However, as both men were known to the lighthouse keeper to be good swimmers he was sure they would climb on the bottom of the upturned boat until help arrived.

The lighthouse keeper didn't have a motor boat so he rowed into St. Jacques a mile distant, and got the local doctor who had a motor yacht to go to the assistance of the men in the overturned boat.

By the time they were ready to go it was nearly dark, so they lit the running lights on the yacht and started off. In the meantime, news of the accident had been telegraphed to the neighbouring community of Belleoram, and the captain of the coastal boat which was in the port decided to also help in the search for the missing men. The ship got underway and steamed out of Belleoram Harbour.

Then, the second tragedy occurred, and no one could ever explain the mystery. The doctor's boat and the coastal boat met outside Belleoram Harbour, and each helmsman thought from the position of the other's lights that they had the right of way. They steamed at full speed until it was too late, and the coastal boat crashed into the doctor's yacht crushing the lighthouse keeper who was standing in the bow, and sending him and the yacht to the bottom. The doctor was thrown free and although he had some broken ribs managed to swim to shore.

The coastal boat carried on to the overturned motor yacht, as did a number of other crafts from the area, but they found no sign of the bodies of the relieving officer or his pilot. Neither was the body of the lighthouse keeper ever found. An inquiry into the second tragedy showed that the lights on both the doctor's yacht and the coastal boat were correct, and there was no natural explanation for what the helmsmen on both ships had seen.

The witch's curse had fallen with a vengeance, and in after years whenever there was a mention of the triple tragedy, people always remembered the witch's curse, and the story passed into the local folklore of Fortune Bay.

The Harbour Grace
Prophecy

When things go wrong for the town of Harbour Grace, you may still see an old-timer shake his head, and mutter something about the Carfagnini prophecy being fulfilled.

This strange legend is connected with the Most Reverend Dr. Henry Carfagnini, a Roman Catholic prelate who served for eleven years as the second bishop of the diocese of Harbour Grace.

Dr. Carfagnini was a native of Naples, Italy, and came to Newfoundland in 1850 to serve as the president of St. Bonaventure's College, St. John's. In 1869, on the death of Bishop Dalton, the first Roman Catholic Bishop of Harbour Grace, Dr. Carfagnini was consecrated bishop, and named his successor.

His appointment did not sit well with the Irish clergy who then served the small but far flung diocese of Harbour Grace. From the very beginning the Italian born bishop did not get on well with the Irish clergy and laity who were his spirtual subjects.

For the first few years of his episcopacy the differences between him and his flock were kept private. In the spring of 1874 however, the problem between the Bishop and his flock became public when Bishop Carfagnini attempted to take control of the Benevolent Irish Society of Harbour Grace.

The Bishop ordered the executive of the Harbour Grace B.I.S. to give him full control of the society, including its funds. They refused his request, and the Bishop took strong measures to assert his authority.

On March 15, 1874, he issued an episcopal decree claiming that in answer to the request of a large number of B.I.S. members who were unhappy with the current executive of the society, he was dissolving the old society. This done, he immediately set up a new B.I.S. with an executive approved by himself.

The executive and most of the members of the dissolved society disregarded the Bishop's decree. They claimed that the Bishop had no right or legal authority to dissolve their society, and they still refused to hand over either their funds or their clubhouse.

Bishop Carfagnini then played what he considered his trump card. On March 22, 1874 he issued a second ecclesiastical decree. This gave the executive and members of the dissolved society together with their supporters, fifteen days to obey their Bishop and abandon the old society, or they would at the end of the fifteen day period be denied the sacraments of the church. Any clerics who supported the old guard B.I.S. would be immediately suspended from their priestly duties.

Undaunted by this threat, the members of the old B.I.S. refused to obey the Bishop or recognize his edict of excommunication.

The Bishop imposed his edict of excommunication, but the B.I.S. and its supporters fought back. Letters and telegrams flooded the office of Cardinal Alexander Franchi, Prefect of the Sacred Congregation at Rome complaining of Bishop Carfagnini and supporting the B.I.S. members who opposed him.

Cardinal Franchi was astounded at the number of telegrams and letters, and summoned Bishop Carfagnini to Rome to explain his actions.

The Bishop left Newfoundland for Rome in October, 1875, and remained there pressing his case until the spring of 1876. The Harbour Grace Irish kept up their letters and telegrams of protest.

In June, 1876 the Pope, through the Sacred Congregation, ordered Bishop Carfagnini to lift his edict of excommunication, and to leave the B.I.S. alone as it was a lay and not a religious society. In order to make sure that this decision was made public, Bishop Carfagnini was ordered to publish the lifting of the spiritual ban in the *Harbour Grace Standard*, and a letter from Cardinal Franchi also published in the same paper made sure that the decision from Rome was made public.

The Italian Bishop had lost, but he tried to explain that it was all just a silly misunderstanding, and he had not really been reprimanded by Rome. The priests and people of Harbour Grace knew differently, there was Franchi's letter to prove it.

For six more years Bishop Carfagnini remained at Harbour Grace. Then in perhaps an attempt to get even with the Irish priests whom he felt had betrayed him, he appointed an Italian priest to a senior parish that became vacant.

It was too much. The Irish priests and their supporters again flooded the office of the Sacred Congregation with telegrams and letters. The Cardinal Prefect had enough, it was obviously time for Bishop Carfagnini's removal. He was appointed to the Sea of Gallipoli in Italy.

On May 27, 1880 a liner called at Harbour Grace to take the Bishop to Europe. It was on this day that the legend of the Harbour Grace Prophecy was born.

It was reported that as the liner moved out the harbour, Bishop Carfagnini stood on her deck, and took a last look at the scene of his first episcopal labours. As the town began to fade from view, he turned to those around him, and prophesied that never again would the town of Harbour Grace prosper. Instead, slowly but surely it would fall into oblivion, and become little more than a ghost town.

Such is the origin of the legend of the Harbour Grace Prophecy.

The Legend of
Father Duffy's Well

n the Salmonier Line about ten miles from the Trans Canada Highway there is a tiny provincial park. The reason for the park's existence is a small well, long known to the travellers of this area as *Father Duffy's Well*. The story of how this well came to be has become a noted Newfoundland legend.

Father James Duffy, for whom the well is named, was a priest from County Monaghan, Ireland, who became the first Roman Catholic pastor of St. Mary's Bay in 1834. In attempting to build a new church at St. Mary's, in 1835, Father Duffy came into conflict with the local magistrate, an Englishman named John Hill Martin who ordered him not to build on the site he had chosen.

Father Duffy built a new church in defiance of the magistrate. Martin then had a large fish flake built around the church that almost cut off access to it.

An enraged Father Duffy countered by ordering his parishioners to cut down and burn the flake under the terrible threat that any who didn't take part would have "*the curse of the congregation fall on them, and the Devil go with them to the grave.*" The flake was cut down.

Acting on the advice of his friend, Chief Justice Bolton known as the *hanging judge*, Martin had Father Duffy and eight St. Mary's men charged in the Newfoundland Supreme Court with riot and sedition.

Father Duffy was arrested and charged, then two policemen went to St. Mary's to arrest the other eight offenders. The eight men, aided by the other men of St. Mary's resisted arrest, and assaulted the two policemen who were forced to flee for their lives.

The Governor then asked for a British warship to come and restore order at St. Mary's. However, before this could happen Father Duffy, after being released from jail, persuaded the eight men to go with him to St. John's and give themselves up. Father Duffy had studied law before joining the church, and he promised to defend the eight St. Mary's men and himself in the Supreme Court.

In March they set out across the trackless bogs and swamps for St. John's. After walking all day they decided to camp for the night. Footsore and weary they made camp, but when they looked around they couldn't find any water to fill their kettle. The men grumbled and complained about this new hardship, but Father Duffy, like Moses in the wilderness, went to a large rock that stood nearby and struck it with his walking stick, and water bubbled up. The men were amazed, and were sure it was a sign of the miraculous power of their priest. They boiled their kettle, roasted their salt fish, and went to sleep confident that Father Duffy would see them through their ordeal.

They were right, Father Duffy won the case and all hands were acquitted. They returned home and told the story of how Father Duffy struck the rock and water bubbled up.

Later, when a road was built to St. Mary's Bay it followed the trail that Father Duffy and the St. Mary's men had blazed across the bogs, and through the forests on their memorable trek to St. John's.

The new road passed right by the *miraculous spring*. Gradually it became a favourite resting place for travellers, and the story of its miraculous discovery and cures were told and retold. Soon people began to carry water from the well to sick relatives, and many are the cures attributed to its sacred water.

Up until 1938, the well was a natural spring, and only a rough board nailed to a nearby tree gave the name as *Father Duffy's Well*. In 1938, the Knights of Columbus built the present wall and piped the water from the spring. In 1958, it became a provincial park. To this very day people still stop at the well to drink its healing waters.

* * * * *

Father Duffy left Newfoundland in 1841, and after a rather stormy stay in Guysborough, Nova Scotia, moved on to Kelly's Cross, Prince Edward Island. Here he died in 1859, and was buried under the church he had built.

Forty-one years later on September 15, 1900, his body was removed from its resting place to make way for a road. When the undertaker, Mr. Hagan and a number of other people opened his casket, they found that Father Duffy's body had not decayed, but was still in a perfect state of preservation.

Father Duffy had always been kindly remembered in Kelly's Cross and now his old parishioners were sure he was a saint. Far away in St. Mary's Bay, Newfoundland, the people had earlier reached the same conclusion, and the story of his *miraculous well* had long since passed into the folklore of the area.

THE ANGEL PRIEST

Around the middle of the last century, Father James Brown, the first native born priest to be ordained and serve in Newfoundland, was the only Roman Catholic priest stationed on the north east coast of Newfoundland. His large parish extended from Green Bay to Labrador. A good man, he did his best to bring the consolation of religion to all his far flung parishioners, and travelled far in all kinds of weather—by boat in summer, and dog and komatic in winter.

At this time the custom of saying Midnight Mass on Christmas Eve was new to Newfoundland. However, Father Brown decided to have a Midnight Mass in his parish church.

To mark the occasion he organized a church choir, and encouraged the people to decorate the church with wreaths of fresh boughs. As Christmas Eve approached the crib was set up, and everything was ready for the big event. The people of the community eagerly looked forward to the novelty of attending church at midnight to start off the Christmas season, and a capacity congregaton was guaranteed.

The day before Christmas Eve, Father Brown got a sick call

to a neighbouring community some miles distant. He set out immediately, but promised the people he would be back in the parish centre for Midnight Mass on Christmas Eve.

However, the weather changed and a violent storm blew up making travel in the area impossible. The people of the parish centre hoped against hope that the weather would clear and the priest would get back for Midnight Mass. But when night fell and he still hadn't returned the people resigned themselves to having the Rosary recited at midnight.

A good crowd gathered in the church around midnight, and one of the older men was about ready to go up to the altar rail to start the Rosary when the sacristy door opened, and a young priest, fully vested for mass, approached the altar.

He was a stranger to the people, but welcomed them to their first Midnight Mass in the name of their pastor, and said that because the good Father was delayed by the storm he would celebrate Midnight Mass with them.

The choir began to sing, and the strange priest joined in with them. Never had the people heard such a voice, it seemed to them that he sang with the voice of an angel.

It was a beautiful mass, and when towards the end of the liturgy the priest turned and blessed the congregation, a strange thrill ran through those who gathered there. After the final Deo gratias and prayers after mass, the strange priest and the altar boys left the altar.

With the natural courtesy of the old time Newfoundlander, a number of men went to the sacristy to thank the strange priest, and wish him Merry Christmas. He was not there, the altar boys said he had disrobed quickly and gone out the back door. The men assumed he was a bit shy and had gone back to the parish house.

The weather cleared up that night, and at daylight on Christmas Day Father Brown left for home. He was sorry that his congregation had missed their Midnight Mass, and it meant he would now have to offer an extra mass to make up for it. Coming to the community he stopped at the house of the parish man, and asked him to go and ring the church bells to summon the people to the first mass.

"You don't need to have an early mass, Father," the man said, "your friend, the young priest, said Midnight Mass for you last night."

"My friend," said the old priest in surprise. "what are you talking about?"

The man told him about the strange priest, and mentioned the beautiful singing. "Everyone said, Father, he had the voice of an angel."

The old priest thought for a moment. The nearest Roman Catholic priest was more than one hundred miles away. Then he knew, God in his mercy had sent an angel to help him out and to reward the faith of his people. He didn't tell the parish man what he was thinking, only wished him a "Holy and Happy Christmas" and went on.

He went straight to the church, and kneeling before the altar thanked God for sending an angel to help an old man keep his word.

He didn't tell the people about the miracle, except to tell them that God had blessed them in ways that were beyond the understanding of mortal men. He did, however, towards the end of his life tell the story of the *angel priest* to a few close clerical friends, and it was only from these people that the legend of the angel priest of the northeast coast has been preserved and passed down to us.

SECTION FOUR

Ghost Stories

THE THREE CORPSES

any years ago on the Port au Port Peninsula, three young men were returning to their homes after attending a dance in a neighbouring community. It was after midnight, and anxious to get home the young men took a short cut through an old cemetery.

Half way through the overgrown grave mounds they suddenly came upon three young women kneeling before a large headstone. Liquor had made the fellows a bit brave, and thinking that they were girls from the community trying to scare them, they approached the kneeling women who seemed to be unaware of their presence.

The boldest of the three spoke to the kneeling women, asking them what they were doing praying in the cemetery at such a late hour. The women paid no attention, but kept their silent vigil.

At this, one of the group became a little uneasy and drew back a bit. "Let's get out of here," he said, "perhaps they're ghosts."

"Ghosts," said the fellow who had spoken to the women, "there's no such thing as ghosts, my son," and to prove his point, he pulled off the hat the nearest girl was wearing and laughingly ran off towards home. The others quickly followed him.

The fellow who had taken the hat threw it in his closet when he got home, and went to bed. The next morning he decided he would take the hat back to the neighbouring community and find its owner.

He went to the closet, but on opening the door uttered a scream of terror for there grinning up at him was a human skull.

The young man was terrified at the sight, and slamming the closet door shut went off to seek the advice of an old woman, the village mid-wife, who was greatly respected for her wisdom. He told her of the midnight meeting in the cemetery, and described the girl he had taken the hat from. The old woman listened carefully, and then gave the name of the girl, adding, "But my son she has been dead these thirty years or more. I helped to lay her out, and put her in her coffin."

"What shall I do?" the young man pleaded. "I really didn't mean any harm, I thought it was some girls playing a trick on us, but I've got to get clear of that skull."

"Yes," said the old woman, "you will have to return it to the dead girl tonight, but I will help you."

"Tonight at midnight, open your closet and you will find the skull is again a hat. Take it with you to the cemetery, and place it back on the head of the ghost whose repose you have broken."

She turned, and opening a small drawer took out a small wooden cross. "Wear this cross on your neck all the while you are in the cemetery and you will be safe."

The young man thanked her, and at midnight as she had ordered, he opened the closet door. Sure enough the skull had disappeared and the hat lay in its place.

He took it up with a shudder, and made his way alone to the cemetery in the neighbouring town. Sure enough, there were the three dead women kneeling before the grave marker and as on the previous night, one of them was bareheaded.

The young man nervously approached the group, and with trembling hands placed the hat back on the head of the girl he had taken it from.

Without warning she sprang to her feet, her eyes blazing with an unearthly fire, and she spoke. "Wretch! You are lucky that you wear the holy emblem on your neck. If you did not, then tonight you would have joined me in my tomb."

At these words the young man turned and fled, and never again did he ever dare to cross a cemetery after dark.

THE HAUNTED PALACE
OF TORS COVE

or many years a very good, but very eccentric priest was the spiritual ruler of the parish of Tors Cove on the Southern Shore.

He lived in a beautiful, old rambling house that he had built when he came to the parish of Tors Cove as a young priest. It had hand-carved mouldings and a circular oak staircase. The local people didn't call it the Rectory or the Presbytery, to them it was the *Palace*, and from his Palace the good Father tended to the spiritual, and sometimes the temporal, needs of his flock for nearly half a century.

According to local legend he was a fearless man who didn't hesitate to chide the vanities of his more well-to-do parishioners right from the pulpit, or to publicly show his contempt for some particular change of ritual demanded by his Archbishop.

On one memorable occasion having received an episcopal order that annoyed him, he dressed a fellow in a mitre, and having read the offending document as commanded by his Archbishop, he came down from the pulpit, and gave the fellow with the mitre a kick in the rear to show what he thought of bishops and their new fangled ideas.

According to many old-timers, he not only ministered to the needs of the living, but sometimes also to the dead. Following sudden disasters at sea, dead men were said to have come seeking absolution, and they were fearlessly received by the intrepid priest.

At the end of a long life he died, and his Palace was rented out to a stranger. However, it was soon apparent that his spirit had stayed in the Palace, for after his funeral people occasionally saw him come in and sit in his favourite chair, light up his pipe, and quickly fill the room with the sweet scent of his favourite pipe tobacco.

There were stories, also, of lights seen in the church at unearthly hours, and of the dead priest leading ghostly congregations in prayer. On these occasions a side door in the Palace that gave a quick access to the church was always found open, even though it had been nailed shut following the death of the priest. After this happened several times the new tenant got the message, and left the door for the use of his ghostly fellow resident.

He was not an unfriendly ghost, and didn't seem to mind sharing his former home with its new inhabitants. However, living in a haunted Palace did have its drawbacks for the tenants, for after the ghost manifested himself a few times to some tradesmen who came to do repairs, not a carpenter, plumber or electrician from the area would be caught dead there. One poor man looked up from his work to find the good Father standing near him sizing up his work. He fled the place not bothering even to take his tools.

The tenant on the other hand did not mind the ghostly presence. He tried to buy the place, but was told it wasn't for sale by the church authorities. When he couldn't buy the Palace the first tenant gave notice and moved out. The house was never rented again. It was closed up for a number of years, and gradually fell into disrepair, until at last it was stripped of its beautiful old furniture and demolished.

All through those desolate times, the old priest's ghost wandered the house at will, doing ill to none, but nevertheless frightening those who saw him.

Where did his ghost seek shelter following the destruction of his home? No one knows for sure, but many people feel that his spirit still haunts the site of his earthly labours, perhaps finding sanctuary in the old church he loved so well.

THE SEALER'S GHOST

round 1875, when sealing was still an important part of the Newfoundland fishery, a man from one of the northern outports got berths for himself and his teenage son on a St. John's sealing vessel.

It was a long trek to St. John's to join the sealing ship, but the young boy didn't mind the hardships. *Going to the ice* was the dream of every young Newfoundlander of the time, and those unlucky enough not to secure a berth often went as stowaways.

They made it to St. John's and boarded their ship. With all flags flying, and to the cheers of the large crowd of spectators who had gathered to watch the sealing fleet leave, they steamed proudly out the *Narrows*.

The first week of the voyage was uneventful. After that it was hard and dangerous work, but the youngster did his part well, and his father was proud of him. Then disaster struck. While getting ready to go over the side, the boy's father suddenly fell to the deck, and when his son tried to help him up he discovered that he was dead.

There was nothing anyone could do. The man was dead but the voyage had to go on. As was the custom with death on a sealing ship, they wrapped the body in a winding sheet filled with salt, placed a cloth over the face, and poured a jug of rum over it. The body was then placed in a rough coffin, which was lashed down on the deck of the ship. The burial would take place on their arrival back in port.

For a day the boy was grief-stricken and mourned the death of his father. However, realizing that he was now the breadwinner of his family, he put his grief aside and threw himself totally into the seal hunt.

The rest of the crew watched as the youngster matched the best of them. There was no place too dangerous to go, and no load too heavy for him to carry. He was first off the ship at dawn and last back at dark. They nodded their approval, and said how proud his poor father would have been of him.

One evening with a storm threatening, he wandered quite a distance from the ship in pursuit of a small seal patch. Intent on the hunt, he didn't notice the weather closing in until having made his kill he turned to go back to the ship. It was hard going, the swirling snow blocked his vision, the wind cut into his flesh, but on he trudged with his haul of pelts. The storm grew worse, and he wandered in a circle, coming back to the place where he had left the seal carcasses.

He began to tire and stopped again to rest, but remembering his dead father's advice "never go to sleep on the ice", he pushed on, but soon he had to rest again. Huddling in the shelter of some rafted ice, he felt the cold begin to fade, and a delicious sense of warmth began to steal over him. He started to grow drowsy but fought against it.

It was then it happened. Out of the swirling snow came the figure of a man, and as he came closer the boy suddenly started up, all sleep banished from his eyes. It was his dead father who was lying wrapped in salt in the makeshift coffin on the deck of the sealing ship. There could be no mistake, his father's features were clear, and unmistakable.

He didn't speak or touch the boy, but beckoned with his hand for him to follow as he turned and walked head on into the blinding blizzard. The boy stood up and followed him, trudging along behind the ghostly figure that kept close to him, but never let him catch up. When the boy began to falter the figure urged him on, and he found the strength to keep going.

When it seemed he couldn't go a step further, the lights of his ship appeared through the swirling snow. He looked for the figure of his father but it had vanished, he was alone on the ice.

He made it to the ship, and was welcomed back as one from the dead. The captain and crew had feared they would have to report a double tragedy to the widow back home.

When he told his story of how his father had come to him on the ice and guided him home, there were no disbelievers. These men had often heard similar stories of a dead loved one leading a person out of danger.

After he had eaten and was rested, the boy quietly went alone to the rough coffin lashed to the deck near the hause pipe, and kneeling by it thanked his dead father for his loving care even after death.

The voyage ended shortly thereafter, and the ship returned to St. John's. It was a bumper trip, and the captain, with the crew's consent, put aside enough money for the body of the dead sealer to be taken home for burial.

Needless to say for the rest of his life the son tended his father's grave with loving care, and long after the son's death, the grave marker told the strange story of his rescue on the ice.

THE HAUNTED HOUSE ON
BAY BULLS ROAD

round 1910 there was a house on Bay Bulls Road, near St. John's, that was avoided by all who had to travel that way after dark. The old farmhouse stood by itself in a field, and was reported to be haunted by a ghostly presence that had driven several families fleeing from the place in terror. It had been deserted for a number of years, but persons caught near the place around midnight told of seeing flames issue from the windows, accompanied by the most ghastly groans and moans.

It was whispered by the old-timers that many years before a very wicked person had entered into a pact with the Devil, and that the flames seen coming from the windows were the very fires of Hell where he was now confined for his evil deeds.

In May of 1917, a group of trouters returning late in the evening to St. John's after a day's fishing in some nearby ponds got caught in a heavy rainstorm near the haunted farmhouse. It was a cold rain driven by an easterly wind, and the trouting party was soon wet and shivering in their drenched clothing. They knew the story of the haunted house, but the rain became so heavy, that four of the younger members of the party decided they would seek shelter there until the storm blew over. The older men would have nothing to do with entering the place, and pushed on to seek shelter further down the road.

The four young men laughed at their companions' fears and ran for the haunted house. They soon had a fire going in the kitchen stove and dried their wet clothing. Then, they settled down to wait out the storm. All evening the wind howled in the chimney, and the rain beat harder and harder against the windows. The four intruders decided to make a night of it and go home in the morning.

They made themselves as comfortable as they could, and tried to get some sleep. Then, exactly at midnight they found out why people gave the place a wide berth. Loud groans seemed to issue from an upstairs room followed by the unmistakable odour of brimstone. A moment later there was a loud clap of thunder, and a human figure wrapped completely in fire appeared in the kitchen. Flames leapt around the room and out through the windows, while the most ghastly howls and shrieks of agony came from the burning figure.

The four fishermen cowered on the floor totally paralysed by the terrifying sight. The glowing figure seemed to pass right through the house, which shivered and shook on its foundation. After a few seconds the burning figure returned, and the cowering visitors could feel the heat of the flames that licked all around them. This time it disappeared as it passed through the walls of the house.

The four young men wasted no time grabbing their belongings and fleeing the place. Needless to say, they never sought shelter there again.

A couple of years later, the old farmhouse was sold, taken down and rebuilt in another community, and the strange phenomenon was never seen again.

THE THING FROM THE SEA

U p until the passing of child welfare laws in Newfoundland, it was not unusual for young boys of eleven or twelve on the death of their fathers to become the sole supporters of their families. The main means of gainful employment in those days was the fishery, and it was as *quartersharemen* in a trap crew or *kedgy* on a banker that these children found employment.

It happened that in the last decade of the last century a man from Holyrood was drowned, leaving behind a wife and two children, the oldest a boy of twelve.

The death of his father ended the boy's school days and his mother looked about for a berth in the trap fishery for him.

She had no luck in finding one in Holyrood, but a trap skiff owner in Brigus agreed to take him for the summer voyage. This meant that the boy would be away from home until the trap season was over.

He said good-bye to his mother and younger brother, and went off to Brigus. The trap crew at Brigus were all young fellows in their late teens or early twenties. The skiff owner had converted an old two storey shed down by the water into a rough bunk house where the men slept, while they ate their meals in the owner's house.

The young boy from Holyrood got on well enough with the rest of the crew, and was doing okay as a trap fisherman.

In early July, a family member of one of the trap crew got married at Cupids. All the crew members were invited to the wedding, but the twelve year old felt he was a bit too young to go. He said he would rather stay alone in the bunk house while the others went to the wedding spree. They didn't expect to get back to Brigus until well after daylight.

The men left for the wedding spree early in the evening, and when it got dark the boy decided to go to bed. He didn't feel scared or anything, although he missed the company of the other men, and had no trouble going to sleep. Later he awakened with a strange feeling that something was wrong. He didn't know what time it was for he had no watch, but it was pitch black in the loft of the old bunk house.

He lay there wondering what time it was and what had awakened him. Then he heard it — a funny noise, a sort of *slurpy, swishy* sound coming from the direction of the ocean and growing louder. He sat up in bed and listened very carefully. It was getting closer — the *swishy, slurpy* sound of someone walking in boots filled with water.

Suddenly, he was afraid. The hair on the back of his neck began to rise. His heart thumped and thumped in his chest. He wanted to jump from the bed and run, but it was as if he was frozen to the spot. The sound grew louder and louder, the door to the shed opened, and it was coming up the ladder to the sleeping loft, *squish, squash.* It came towards the bed. He was paralysed with fright.

As the unknown thing from the sea approached the bed, the boy was aware of the pungent smell of salt water mixed with kelp and decaying seaweed. He then felt it climbing on the mattress. A strand of cold wet hair fell across his face, and a bony hand touched his forehead.

The touch of the thing broke the spell that had bound him to the bed. With a scream of horror, he leaped from the bed, tumbled down the ladder, and fled to the house of the trap skiff owner at the top of the lane. Here the trap crew found him the next morning when they got back from the wedding spree. He was crouched behind the stove, hardly able to speak.

After a while, he managed to tell them the whole frightful story, shivering at the memory of his night of horror. The owner of the skiff told him it wasn't the first time someone had met the unknown creature from the sea. No one had any idea of what it was or the purpose of its nocturnal visits to the shed.

The boy wasn't sure whether or not he could sleep in that loft again, but remembering he was the sole supporter of his widowed mother and little brother he put on a bold face, and said he didn't mind going back as long as the rest of the trap skiff crew were there too.

They then had breakfast, and just as they finished there was the sound of cart wheels outside the door. A few minutes later the boy's mother entered looking for her son.

She too had a strange story to tell — a terrible dream that had brought her to see her son. The night before she had awakened at two o'clock with a terrible feeling that some danger threatened her son. So strong was the dream that she couldn't rest until she had talked with him. When daylight broke she borrowed her neighbour's horse and cart and left to see him.

On hearing his story she didn't hesitate, but took the frightened boy back to Holyrood with her. A few days later he got a berth with a Holyrood trap crew, and was able to support his family once again.

However, he never forgot the *Thing from the Sea* and was curious as to what it wanted. Some years later as a young man he went back to Brigus with the intention of spending another night alone in the shed loft. This time if the unknown creature came out of the sea he intended to ask who it was and what it wanted?

He was too late for a mysterious fire had destroyed the shed a few years previous. The identity of the *Thing from the Sea* would remain forever a mystery.

SECTION FIVE

Superstitions, Cures and Weather Lore

SUPERSTITIONS IN NEWFOUNDLAND

The early settlers of Newfoundland brought from their countries of origin the superstitions of their ancestors, and added to them in the land of their adoption.

From England, Ireland, Scotland and France came omens of good and ill fortune, and especially omens of impending disasters and death. There are numerous stories about family members seeing a loved one appear suddenly before them when they were far away at sea or on a foreign battlefield. Such sightings were always followed by news of the death of the loved one.

As well, there were certain actions that foretold a coming death in a family. If for instance a person placed a pair of new shoes or boots on a table, then someone near and dear to them would be dead within a year. The same was true if a window blind suddenly fell to the floor, or a lamp chimney shattered. To buy a new broom in the month of May was also an omen of death. There was an old rhyme that said "Buy a new broom in May and you'll sweep your best friend away".

Counteracting the bad luck omens were those that foretold good fortune. Finding a horseshoe in the street or a four leaf clover in a field meant the best of luck for the future. If the *fetch* of a person was seen going towards their home it was a sign of a long life for that person. Wearing a hole in the sole of your right shoe was a sure sign that you would be wealthy before you died.

Besides a belief in these omens of good and bad luck, there was also a strong belief in the presence of demons, witches and wizards in Newfoundland. In many communities there were men and women whose curses were greatly feared by their fellow villagers, for they were supposed to be in league with the Devil.

To contact the Devil in order to become one of his disciples there were certain very secret rituals that had to be performed. One of these rituals that seems to have originated from Cornwall began with attendance at church. "Let the person go to chancel, to sacrament, and let him hide and bring away the bread from the hands of the priest. Next midnight let him or her take it, and carry it around the church *widdershins*, that is from south to north crossing to east three times. The third time a big, ugly venomous toad gaping and gasping with his mouth open wide will meet him or her. Let the person put the bread between the lips of the ghastly creature, and as soon as it is swallowed he will breathe three times upon the person, and he or she will be made a witch for evermore."

In another Newfoundland tradition concerning witchcraft, the *dark power* once granted was passed down in an unbroken line reaching back as far as people could remember. Certain local witches built up such a reputation for knowing the future that people came from far away to consult with them.

In an article on "Superstitions in Newfoundland", H.F. Shortis a noted Newfoundland historiographer tells the story of John O'Dwyer, a planter of Fogo. He built a new schooner but after the launching he had nothing but bad luck. Convinced that the schooner had a curse on her he went up to St. John's to see a rather famous witch who lived near Jobs Lane. The witch looked into his future and told him he had built a coffin for himself. John O'Dwyer went home and let the new schooner rot at her mooring.

Even today in certain parts of Newfoundland there is a firm belief in the presence of witches in the community, and a healthy respect for their *dark power*.

Another old Newfoundland superstition was the belief that certain spirits of the dead could not go peacefully into eternity but had to stay on earth to expiate some secret crime. According to an old superstition these unquiet spirits sometimes took refuge in an old tree, and woe to the person who attempted to cut it down.

Such a tree stood for many years in a clearing in the Spring Meadow area of Terrenceville, Fortune Bay. It was a gnarled, old spruce that was said to be more than one hundred years old, and looked like it had been struck by lightening. Legend had it that many years ago a man had attempted to cut down the tree for firewood. This so angered the spirit who made his home in the tree, that he turned the man's axe against him, and he barely escaped with his life.

There was also an old superstition about opening your doors after midnight on a stormy night, for by so doing you could let in some restless spirit who might be seeking shelter from the storm. Once in, it might be difficult to dislodge your unwanted guest.

Some Newfoundland Cures, Charms and Healers

n the days when doctors were few and hospitals non existent, the people of Newfoundland depended on natural healers, charms and various folk medicine to cure their ills.

The Old Hag

One of the greatest afflictions of the Newfoundland male of those far off times was the visitation of the *Old Hag*. This strange nightmarish creature came in your sleep and put you in a semiconscious state, where you lay half-way between sleeping and waking.

She sat on your chest and tried to choke the life out of you. The agony suffered was terrible, and there was nothing the victims could do to help themselves. If afflicted, the only hope was that someone else would become aware of your problem through your moaning and groaning, and call your name backwards. This drove the Old Hag away, and let you wake up. However, this only worked if you had company.

A man from Change Islands was terribly afflicted by the Old Hag who came and tormented him nearly every night, until he was afraid to go to sleep. At last in desperation he went to an old man who was very knowledgeable in dealing with sickness of every kind.

He had a very effective remedy for the victim.

"Take a shingle," he said, "and drive it full of sharp nails, then strap the shingle to your breast with the nails pointing out, and go to bed."

Following the old man's advice, the man prepared a shingle, and having put it in place got in his bed. He soon drifted off to sleep, and as usual the Old Hag came and flopped down on his chest, but on connecting with the nails, she let out a series of horrid screams and flew away much faster than she had come. The man was never bothered by the Old Hag again.

Dog Bites

One of the strange cures for the bite of a dog was to kill the offending animal and take its liver and fasten it to the wound.

Toothache

This *hell of a disease* as it was called in Newfoundland, was one of the greatest scourges of the times and people resorted to desperate remedies.

One well known cure in Trinity Bay was to carry a copy of a certain letter to *Abzarus, King of Edessa* for fourteen days.

In Fortune Bay, one cure was to tie seven knots in a piece of string and wear it on your wrist. Sometimes desperate people used gun powder and lye to burn out the offending molar.

At King's Cove, the scraping of some dust from a tombstone and placing on the sore tooth was an instant cure. In other places they take a few pebbles from a new made grave and while touching the afflicted area, they invoked the Trinity.

The Dogberry Tree

It was a common belief in nineteenth century Newfoundland that if a child was passed through the branches of a dogberry tree it would prevent them from getting measles, smallpox, ricketts and childhood diseases.

At Wesleyville, Bonavista Bay, there was for more than a hundred years a very ancient dogberry tree known as *Uncle Joe Tiller's Tree*. It was fenced in, and considered sacred by the inhabitants of the town for legend had it that once a hunchback child was passed through a crook in the tree, and was cured. Most of the children of Wesleyville were passed though its branches.

There were similar trees in many other Newfoundland outport communities.

The Cahill's Gift

According to an ancient tradition certain members of the Cahill clan have the gift of healing the disease known as *St. Anthony's Fire*.

The legend says that when Christ was on his way to Calvary, a member of the Cahill clan helped Him in some way, and this special gift of healing was bestowed on him and his descendants.

In the town of St. Mary's, St. Mary's Bay, a resident by the name of Stan Cahill was known far and wide for his ability to cure the ravages of St. Anthony's Fire, and people came from far and near to get his help.

The procedure he used was simple, but very effective. When a victim of St. Anthony's Fire came to him, Stan Cahill would prick his thumb with a needle and smear a drop of blood on the place where the person had the burning and swelling caused by St. Anthony's Fire. Sometimes the patient would have to make a couple of trips, but the cure was never known to fail.

The Seventh Son of A Seventh Son

This person was supposed to have the power to cure epilepsy, and other diseases through the power of his touch. To see if the person had this power, you put a live worm on the palm of their hand. If they had the power to cure, the worm would shrivel up and die, if it lived, the person was a charlatan.

Charm for Stopping Bleeding

You say the name of the person or animal to be helped. The charm will not work if the name is not repeated twice. Then, you say the verse from *Ezekiel* in the King James version of the Bible, beginning "I said to thee when thou wast in thy blood live", and so on to the end of that verse. The verse, like the name of the person must be repeated twice to be effective.

Warts

There were many and various cures for warts, among them the following:

Find a person who was willing to buy your warts. They gave you a coin for them, and in time they would all disappear.

Take a piece of bread and prick the wart until it starts to bleed, then smear a little blood on the bread. Throw it out, and when the birds or an animal eat the bread, then you warts will disappear.

Take a piece of chalk and mark an *X* with the chalk on the wart. With the same piece of chalk mark an *X* on the stove, when the chalk mark on the stove was burnt away then the wart you had marked would disappear.

Whooping Cough

Find a woman married to a man with the same surname as herself, and get her to give you a slice of bread and butter. The cough will be cured.

Rheumatism

A sure cure for rheumatism is to carry a potato in your pocket.

NEWFOUNDLAND FOLKLORE
OF THE MONTHS

 ANUARY

Weather Lore

The weather of the first twelve days of January indicates the weather for the next twelve months.

If the wind blows south on New Year's night a warm and sunny year will follow.

If the wind blows west on New Year's Day it foretells a good fishery and a good harvest.

If January is a warm sunny month then there will be snow in May.

Special Days

New Year's Day

Tradition of open house for the general public by leaders of church and state. This was also the day for making your resolutions for the coming year.

Twelfth Day or Old Christmas Day—January 6

Last day for Christmas celebrations, especially going out as mummers. Before they were put down, this was the day for *the fools* to go out.

Superstitions

If the first person to enter your house on New Year's is dark then you will have good luck all the year, but if a fair person comes first it will be an unlucky year.

Any unusual task you perform on New Year's Day you will have to perform often during the coming year.

To work on New Year's Day will bring bad luck all year.

If a friend leaves the gift of a coin at your house you will have money all year.

FEBRUARY

Weather Lore

If Candlemas Day (February 2) is fair and fine
The worst of the winter is left behind.
If Candlemas Day is dark and grum,
The worst of the winter is still to come.

If February gives much snow,
A fine summer it doth foreshow.

If the wind's in the east on Candlemas Day
There it will stick 'till the end of May.

If Candlemas Day is fine a good fishery and harvest is assured.

Special Days

Feast of St. Brigid—February 1

Candlemas Day—February 2

Candles were blessed in the parish church. To have one of those candles would protect your house from fire during the rest of the year.

Feast of St. Blaise—February 3

Saint Valentine's Day—February 14

This was the day for lovers to exchange presents, and friends to give valentines.

Superstitions

If you put a piece of string outside the house on the Eve of St. Brigid, the Saint will walk on it. You take it in the next morning, and it then becomes a safeguard against all falls or accidents from stumbling if the string is worn around the ankle.

If a girl decorated her pillow with five bay leaves on St. Valentine's Eve (February 13) and dreamed of her lover, then she would be married within a year.

The first person of the opposite sex that you met on Valentine's Day was destined to be your husband or wife.

Customs

Gifts were exchanged between sweethearts, and children exchanged valentines with all their friends and neighbours. The valentines were usually home-made and anonymous. The number of valentines you got on this day showed your popularity. Sometimes it was an opportunity to say something nasty about an enemy through an anonymous valentine.

ARCH

Weather Lore

If March comes in like a lamb
It will go out like a lion.

A peck of March dust is worth a king's ransom.

If St. Patrick's Day (March 17) is fair and sunny then St. Patrick will take the cold stone from the water and there will be an early and warm spring.

Special Day

St. Patrick's Day—March 17

This is the big day for the Newfoundland Irish. Even in the old days the Lenten fast didn't apply to St. Patrick's Day for Roman Catholics and they could eat, drink and make merry to their heart's content. Plays, concerts and dances were held in all communities where there were people of Irish descent.

APRIL

Weather Lore

If the first three days in April be foggy,
Rain in June will make the grass boggy.
April showers will bring May flowers.

Special Days

All Fools Day—April 1

From early morning until twelve noon practical jokes were the order of the day. If someone played an April Fool's joke after midday you put them down with:

April Fool is gone apast
You're the biggest fool at last,
Up the ladder, down the tree,
You're a bigger fool than me.

St. George's Day—April 23

This is the special day for all of English descent, the equivalent of St. Patrick's Day to those of Irish descent. It is kept as a provincial holiday on the nearest Monday.

AY

Weather Lore

Mists in May, heat in June.

Special Day

Queen's Birthday — May 24

It is now called Victoria Day. Newfoundland tradition is that you must *wet a line* on Queen Victoria's birthday. It marks the beginning of the trek to the summer homes and cottages in Newfoundland. It is a school and public holiday.

Twenty-fourth of May
The Queen's birthday,
If we don't get a holiday
We'll all run away.

UNE

Weather Lore

A dripping June brings all things in tune.

If St. Vitus Day (June 15) is rainy weather
It will rain for thirty days together.

If June 8 is wet there will be a wet harvest.

Special Day

St. John's Day — June 24

At one time bonfires were lit on the headlands, but this custom died away. Today St. John's Day is a public holiday in Newfoundland and there are celebrations in the city of St. John's.

Superstitions

A girl who puts an egg in a tumbler before noon, and then

throws it out in the street after noon, can find the initials of the man she is to marry by watching the first man to walk over the place where she threw the egg.

A second way to do this was to boil an egg on the morning of St. John's Day, then remove half the egg from the shell and fill with salt. You put the salted egg next to your bed, and sometime during the night your future husband would come to you in a dream.

A third way was to break an egg in a tumbler and put it in the window. As the egg settled, in some mysterious way the girl would find out when and whom she would marry.

JULY

Weather Lore

If it rains on St. Swithin's Day (July 15) then it will rain a little every day for the forty days following.

Special Days

Remembrance Day—July 1

A holiday declared in memory of the Newfoundlanders who died in the July Drive. After Confederation it was a dual celebration as Remembrance Day and Dominion Day.

Orangeman's Day—July 12

A big holiday in Newfoundland and celebrated by members of the Orange Society and their supporters. There were usually parades and dinners to mark the occasion when King Billy crossed the Boyne. There were also some serious fights between the Orange and the Green in a few Newfoundland communities.

UGUST

Weather Lore

Sunshine on St. Mary's Day (August 15) brings good red wine.

If St. Bartlemy Day (August 24) be fair and clear
Hopes for a prosperous autumn that year.

Special Days

Lady Day—August 15

It was a holy day for Roman Catholics. There were usually celebrations to mark the return of the Labrador men on that day, and for some people it was the day that they first dug some new potatoes in their gardens.

Regatta Day

This is St. John's civic holiday to mark the oldest regatta in North America. It has always been a fun day for the people of St. John's and the surrounding area. It is traditionally held on the first Wednesday in the month of August. If weather conditions are unfavourable it is then held on the next calm, fine day. Wind conditions play a major role in this event.

EPTEMBER

Weather Lore

If St. Matthew's Day (September 21) is bright and clear
It means good weather for the coming year.

Special Day

Labour Day

It is the first Monday of September—a public holiday that marks the end of the summer cabin season in Newfoundland. In areas where the labour movement is strong there are sometimes parades and entertainment.

OCTOBER

Weather Lore

When the winds of October won't make the leaves go,
There'll be a frosty winter with banks of snow.

A windy, frosty October means a mild January and February.

Special Days

Hallowe'en — October 31

In early Newfoundland, October 31 was known as *Colcannon Night* or sometimes as *Snap Apple Night*. Colcannon was usually a seven vegetable dish served up for the main meal on that day. All the vegetables were boiled in one pot. Snap apple came from the practice of hanging apples from a beam and trying to get one by jumping up, and trying to get the apple in your mouth.

There was no trick or treating in Newfoundland in the early days. Trick or treating came with the American soldiers in 1941, and spread throughout Newfoundland. It was helped by the coming of American shows on television. Ducking and snapping for apples however, was a fairly common practice on this night during the old days.

Superstitions

On this night if two lovers placed a pair of walnuts on the fire and they lay still and burned together, then it was a sign of a happy future. If however, they flew apart then life together would be a stormy relationship.

If a young girl wanted to see her true love, she would take a candle and an apple and go into a dark room where there was a mirror. If she sat before the mirror, holding a candle in her hand and ate the apple, she would see the face of her lover looking over her shoulder reflected in the mirror.

OVEMBER

Weather Lore

If ducks do slide at Hollantide (November 11)
At Christmas they will swim.

Special Days

All Saints' Day—November 1

This day used to be a *holy day of obligation* for all Roman Catholics in Newfoundland.

All Souls' Day—November 2

Although not a *holy day of obligation* for Roman Catholics this was the day people remembered the souls of the dead. Three masses were celebrated in the churches and special prayers were said for dead relatives.

The souls of the dead who wished to return to earth could return on this night. You never threw out any water after sunset because you might splash the soul of some dear departed one. People kept well away from the graveyard from sunset until the next dawn.

Guy Fawkes Day—November 5

Guy Fawkes night was a big event in the old days. For months rival groups of young people gathered old wood, fish tubs, in fact anything that would burn. The aim was to have the biggest and long lasting fire in your community.

Armistice Day—November 11

This holiday to celebrate the end of World War I and II is still celebrated in Newfoundland.

In the old days bonfires were lit and there were parades in the larger centres with laying of remembrance wreaths which is still done in many places.

DECEMBER

Weather Lore

A warm Christmas is a cold Easter.

A green Christmas, a white Easter.

If there is much wind on Christmas Day there will be a good crop of berries.

A wet Christmas means a poor harvest the coming year.

Special Days

Christmas Eve—December 24

Santa Claus came after midnight. A meal of salt fish was usually served. In some Newfoundland communities it was believed that at midnight all the animals knelt to honour the Saviour.

Christmas Day—December 25

This is the biggest Newfoundland holiday. Everyone tries to be home for this day. One old Christmas custom was to fire off a gun when you had finished your Christmas dinner—a signal you were open for visitors.

There was feasting and mummering and in some communities a dance in the schoolhouse or parish hall.

Holy Innocents Day—December 28

This was considered the most unlucky day in the year in many places in Newfoundland, and few people began any work on this day for it was sure to come to no good.

New Year's Eve—December 31

In Scotland it is called *Hogmanay*. It was considered bad luck to let the fire go out on this night. Sweeping the floor was frowned upon, also, for you might sweep out all your luck for the new year. The birth of a child on this day brought good luck to all the family.

BIBLIOGRAPHY

BOOKS

Bartlett, Bob Capt., *The Log of Bob Bartlett*, New York, 1828.

Byrnes, John M., *The Paths to Yesterday*, Boston, 1931.

Chappell, Edward Lieut., *The Voyage of M.M.S. Rosamond*, London, 1818.

Devine & O'Mara, *Five Thousand Historical Facts About Newfoundland*, St. John's, 1990.

Devine, P.K., *Devine's Folklore of Newfoundland*, St. John's, 1937.

Dodd, Jack Capt., *The Wind in the Rigging*, St. John's, 1971.

England, George; Evans, Alan, *Vikings of the Ice*, New York, 1924.

Evans, Allan, *Splendour of St. Jacques*, St. John's, 1981.

Fitz-Gerals, Conrad Jr., *The Albatross*, Bristol, 1935.

Fitzgerald, L.C. Rev., *Lone Eagles of God*, 2nd. ed., Dublin. (No date of publication given.)

Fitzgerald, Jack, *Newfoundland Believe It or Not*, St. John's, 1974.

Horwood, Harold, *Newfoundland*, Toronto, 1969.

Kinsella, P.J., *Some Superstitions and Traditions of Newfoundland*, St. John's, 1919.

Millais, J.G., *Newfoundland — Its Untrodden Ways*, New York, 1969.

Miller, Florence, *In Caribou Land*, Toronto, 1929.

Murphy, James, *Customs of the Past*, St. John's, 1918.

Murphy, Michael, *Pathways Through Yesterday*, St. John's, 1978.

O'Crohan, *The Islandman*, Oxford University Press, Oxford, 1985.

Reader, H.J., *Newfoundland Wit, Humour and Folklore*, St. John's, 1982.

Smith, J. Harry, *Newfoundland Holiday*, Toronto, 1952.

Toque, Philip Rev., *Newfoundland As It Was and How It Is In 1878*, Toronto, 1878.

Wakeham, P.J., *Twenty Newfoundland Stories*, St. John's, 1953.

Wix, Edward Rev., *Six Months of A Newfoundland Missionary's Journal*, London, 1833.

ARTICLES

Carfagnini, Henry Rt. Rev., "Letter to Ed.", I.C.B.U. Journal, Philadelphia, published by *The Newfoundlander*, St. John's, July 18, 1876.

"Letter" to Very Rev. A.E. Walsh, *Newfoundlander*, July 18, 1876.

Franchi, Alexander Cardinal, "Letter" to Very Rev. A.E. Walsh, *Newfoundlander*, St. John's, July 19, 1876.

Dawe, Thomas, "A Chat About Fairies", *The Newfoundland Quarterly*, Vol. LXVL, No. 3, Summer 1968.

Dickens, Charles, Ed. "Remembrance of a Cornish Vicar", *All The Year Round*, Vol. XIII, March 11, 1865.

McCarthy, M.J., "History of St. Mary's Bay", *Arts and Letters Publication*, St. John's, 1971.

Robertson, B. Dr., "Kelly's Island".

Pirate File, Newfoundland Historical Society Office.

Shortis, H.F., "Superstitions in Newfoundland" (unpublished typescript), Newfoundland Archives, St. John's.

Acknowledgement

We wish to acknowledge and thank the following persons for their help in collecting the material for this book: Art Crocker; Frank Galgay; Mrs. Alice Hamlyn; Gerard Healey; Mrs. Yvonne Humby; Joseph Kinsella; Mrs. Queen Maloney; Mrs. Betty Mandeville; Steve Mandeville; Mrs. Anna McCarthy; Mrs. Clare Pippy; Ernest Pippy; Raymond Tubrett; the staff of the Newfoundland Historical Society office; the staff of the Newfoundland Archives and the staff of the Dr. Hunter Library.

We as publishers have tried to keep these tales in their original form and context as they have been passed down through the ages. Therefore, editing has been kept at a minimum.